SWIMMING IN SILK

Darren Williams grew up on the far north coast of New South Wales. He had long wanted to be a writer and in 1992, Darren took time off work to begin his first novel, *Swimming in Silk*. He describes the process as 'months and months of hard work punctuated by moments of pure exhilaration.'

SWIMMING IN SILK

DARREN WILLIAMS

ALLEN & UNWIN

Publication of this title was assisted by The Australia
Council, the Federal Government's arts funding and
advisory body.

First published in 1995 by
Allen & Unwin Pty Ltd
9 Atchison Street, St Leonards, NSW 2065 Australia

National Library of Australia
Cataloguing-in-Publication entry:

Williams, Darren, 1967– .
  Swimming in silk

  ISBN 1 86373 849 5.
  I. Title

A823.3

Set in 10/13 pt Palatino by DOCUPRO, Sydney
Printed by Australian Print Group, Maryborough, Victoria

10 9 8 7 6 5 4 3 2 1

For Santina

Contents

ONE

The colour of the world

Cliff reeled along the road and followed a light that appeared regularly and magically from the belly of a black cloud. He knew his house lay somewhere between the ocean and the next step he took. Easy.

The night was warm and his glasses slid along his nose until he could barely see where he was going. The country quiet rang in his ears after the din and clamour of the hotel. He could hear his feet hitting the ground but couldn't place the rhythm they made. He heard someone laugh close by and the sound curled into his ears and tickled something there. He stopped and peered through the trees. He could smell something sweet and strange in the air, as if a pair of giddy clowns had, moments before, blended secret ingredients and disappeared themselves in a puff of greasy smoke. He turned off the road and followed the smell and the memory of the laugh. He saw a barbed-wire fence and stopped himself before his body tried to hurdle it. He found a post and, carefully, supporting himself with a shaking arm, climbed the rungs of wire. When he was able to he jumped and sailed free of the fence, but as he reached the ground, his legs buckled and he fell awkwardly on his side and the air was knocked from his chest. He picked himself up, took a deep and slow breath, but felt no pain. He continued walking until the ground sloped down into a gully and he made a path for himself beside the creek he found at the bottom of it. The air around him smelt of earth and rain. He set his feet as carefully as he could and walked until the banks widened and circled a waterhole. He stopped under a tree and squatted and held his knees in his hands.

The pool looked fresh and clean. The creek met the deeper flow of the river further down. Trees hung over the water and dipped their branches in as if to drink. It seemed like a place where rumours were born, where bunyips slept wrapped in weed like kittens, where water eddied and became whirlpools and became storms.

Cliff could see the swimmers. He could hear their voices. He shrank into the shadow of the tree. Something warm dripped from his lip. He could taste it. Blood. Shit. His nose was bleeding again. He didn't think he had bumped it coming over the fence. He couldn't remember bumping it at the pub. He couldn't remember that far back.

He felt faint and his skin prickled and the blood trickled out and merged and thinned in the sweat on his face. Crickets sang in the grass near his feet and hurt his head.

'Shut up!' he whispered to them.

He hoped the bleeding would stop soon. His mouth was dry. He edged down to the creek but stopped when he saw cars parked among the trees on the opposite bank. He moved back to his spot. He could see everything. No one could see him. The girl laughed again, a pure and happy sound that made him close his eyes. What the hell could be so funny?

A fire flickered on the rocky part of the bank and people milled around it. They were tan from the summer sun and some sat roasting themselves by the fire as if they wanted to become even darker. Cliff watched them. He could see the heat jumping through the air and onto their skin. Their eyes were white and glowing in their heads. A girl appeared and her skin was pale and her hair was dark and she laughed and it was the laugh he had heard before. She looked strange among the burnished bodies and sun-blond hair. He watched

4

her face as she laughed again; her body shook, drops of water sliding off her as if she were coated in oil.

She's the happy one, he said to no one.

His heart thudded inside him and he wondered why it did. He felt the press of blood across his head, his face, and felt the drip from his nose, slick and warm. He leaned forward and the earth caught the flow. He needed a cigarette.

He watched the girl. Her body was smooth except for tiny creases creeping out from her armpits as if something lay folded and hidden there inside her. She stood with her hands on her hips and swayed back and forth in the smoke. She was angles and bones and she was drunk. A man he hadn't noticed before watched her and laughed. She stumbled away from the fire and the man followed her. Another girl squealed and laughed as a boy grappled with her and tried to throw her into the water. A slab of rock sloped away from the bank and disappeared like a dull reef into the pool. The boy, his forehead ridged and tight and a beard straggling across his chin, dived into the deep water and taunted the girl as he swam. The pale girl and the man disappeared between the cars. Cliff tried to see where they went. He sank his fingers through leaves and into the soft earth at his feet. He felt something hard and cold and scraped away the earth around it until a piece of metal jutted out like a finger. He bent the piece back and forth until it broke off in his hand. Fire-light traced the broken edge. He threw it away and tried to break more from the piece in the ground but he could feel it becoming thicker the deeper his fingers followed it. He wondered what it was.

The girl and the man did not return to the fire. Darkness fell. Cliff stood and his knees cracked. He turned and headed slowly back to the road. Leaves under his boots muffled his movements. A bird landed in the tree above and startled him. He heard its soft scrape against the branch and the whir of wings as it rested. He lifted his head and looked into the seamless black eye of the bird until it flew away.

Headlights came spearing through the trees, lighting him up where he stood, lighting the bloody stain across his face and down his overalls. He froze and the car's engine roared. He didn't breathe. The car backed away and then stopped. Its engine died and the lights went out. No sound came from the car. No one got out.

Cliff backed away towards the thicker bush. He thought it was okay but as soon as he had taken a second step the car's lights came on again and drenched him, pinned him. Shrieks and howls came from the car as doors slammed.

He ran.

His legs were stiff and shaky from crouching. He was in a dream. He slapped through leaves and branches. He could hear shouting voices behind him. Two, three, four. Shouting abuse and his name. His name rang out. His teeth tingled and he started to giggle and couldn't stop. He broke through the edge of the trees and out into the long grass of the paddock. His muscles felt like brass. The ground sloped upward toward the edge of a larger and darker stand of bush. He ran for it, crossing the open space with long strides. He could hear them coming through the bush behind him. He reached the top of the hill and the trees. He ran between them and fell to the ground and curled his body into a ball in a dark hollow of fern and bush. He heard them coming, each one with blood in their voice as if he had threatened rape against their sisters, mothers, grandmothers. He fought an urge to laugh out loud; held his nose and mouth and squeezed hard. They skirted the bush a few times shouting threats and throwing fallen branches into the blackness but it was too dark for them to see anything. They soon gave up. He heard them walk back down the hill muttering to each other. He looked up and saw their backs, broad and bare. One, two, three, four. Only young. He laughed at them.

'Fucking little shits,' he said. *Fucking little shits.*

He waited and then stepped out into the open and walked

home. He found his house, silent and still, somewhere between the tips of his boots and the sea—just as he knew he would. He sank into a chair. His bones ached. He drank a jug of water. His nose stopped bleeding. He watched television with a piece of wood across his knees in case the bastards decided to visit. He tried not to fall asleep. His favourite shows came on late and he watched them, sobering, in the dark. In the early morning he fell asleep and nothing disturbed him until the sun had climbed high in the sky.

Daniel stared at the map collapsing across his knees and at himself in the mirror, looking at the map. You are an ugly prick, he said to his reflection. He followed the inky lines with his fingers but even that was useless because he didn't know where he was. He sniffed and blew his nose and looked around; no signs, no people. He pushed in the car's cigarette lighter and when it sprang out he placed the orange spiral against the map and burnt a hole in it.

He glanced in the mirror again. He thought he looked pale; blood camped in bloodshot eyes. He threw the map down and rested his head against the seat. His chest hurt. He was convinced he was going to die. It was a beautiful day. That clinched it.

The sky was stacked with white clouds and he watched them drift slowly by. It was like being under surf and looking up; the water churning and foaming, the sun in the water with you like a best friend. He wanted to be there, by the sea, watering his pale body, healing it. Sleeping. But, lost as he was beside a back road, he wondered if he would ever see the ocean again.

He closed his eyes and listened and, for a long time, heard nothing to make him open them. He drifted and imagined jumping on a cloud and riding it to the beach, looking down and watching the country roll by. Maybe tossing lollies to kids he saw or taking them to a circus or something, the best in the world, invisible to grown-ups who would just go on with their business and forget their children ever existed.

He heard a jet churning high overhead, trailing pale finery through the clouds. He opened his eyes and remembered where he was and was not.

A crow jumped onto the road in front of him. Its slick blackness surprised him. It made no sound but sidled along the verge toward the car. It was death again, shifty-eyed, sneaking up. His chest hurt. He started the car and drove off.

The bathroom was cooler than the rest of the house. The tap dripped chrome into the sink. Susan stood under the shower, gritted her teeth and hummed a dumb tune until she had finished. She stepped out onto the tiles and dried herself with the last clean towel in the cupboard.

She switched on the radio for company and sat at the table in the kitchen and watched the city outside get wetter and wetter, gutters overflowing down slippery back walls. She sat and watched and rocked back and forth slowly in the chair. It was past midnight. She was waiting for him to come home.

She looked at her watch and stopped rocking. She jumped up from the table and threw clothes on and more into a suitcase. She hesitated for a moment and then kept on packing. She packed everything she thought she might need until the suitcase was fat and tight. She finished. Panting, she sat down again. She felt better. She smiled and saw her reflection in the pane of the window smile back.

She made herself a mug of coffee and drank it slowly. Her heart began to pound as her ears listened for the sound of him coming home. She stood on trembling legs and found paper and pen. She wrote a note. She tried to think of something cryptic. Something he could ponder over coffee. Finally, she wrote, *See you later*, but she knew it wouldn't be that simple.

She left the house, quickly, before she changed her mind. She slammed the door behind her and threw the suitcase into the car and drove away.

Jade woke and rubbed her eyes. She had dreamt of her father again. She had been looking through a window, across a sleeping town and then the wind had blown through a tree and she had seen him climbing up the wall, his fingers bloody and digging into the boards, a knife sparkling in his mouth, his tongue rubbing against its edge, sawing at its root and him climbing, shifting his weight insect-like up to where she stood, frozen and halfway out the window.

She rubbed her eye. It itched. She was in bed—not her own—and she had to think before she remembered where she was. She could see a man's back, broad and freckled, beside her. She held herself still. The room was bright. She turned towards the window and squinted at the blue sky. Her head ached and her mouth was as dry as dust. She felt nothing between her body and the sheet. She lifted her head but couldn't see her clothes anywhere. She looked at the man sleeping next to her. Russell something. His breathing was ragged. She remembered dogs jumping and licking at her. She rolled off the bed slowly, quietly, so he wouldn't wake. She spotted her clothes in a pile on the floor and she put them on and then looked around for her bag, but couldn't see it. She wanted to run but found she couldn't move at more than a slow sick walk. She thought she should just wake the bastard up and ask him where her bag was but she didn't want to face him; she didn't want him talking to her. She had to go the toilet. She was bursting. She walked through the open bedroom door and into the living room. The house was new and smelt of paint and fresh carpet. Her bag was sitting on the kitchen table. It was open and her belongings were scattered across the table. She put everything back and pulled the draw-string tight. She heard someone snoring. It wasn't Russell but Russell's brother, asleep on the lounge in his underpants, drooling on a pillow.

She walked into the bathroom and sat on the toilet and stared dully at the fresh purple bruises which had appeared along her leg. Her hands trembled. She concentrated on the poster stuck up on the wall. It was a painting of a poodle with long eyelashes wearing a suspender belt and stockings and smoking a cigarette in a holder. She closed her eyes but she could still see it. She stood in front of the mirror and pulled her hair into a tight ponytail at the back. She opened the bathroom door and walked across the room with her eyes fixed on the brother. She couldn't remember his name. He was still snoring. Scattered on the floor in front of him were photographs. She could see what they were of from where she stood. She remembered and she shivered and stepped toward him, barely breathing, and bent and picked up each one. She crossed the room to the front door and opened it and walked outside and started to breathe again. Two barking dogs appeared from the back of the house. She jumped and they jumped up and danced around her on their back legs. The noise hurt her head. She walked to the front gate and stood trying to undo the catch of twisted wire. She heard the front door open behind her and a shouting voice but she kept struggling, her fingers dull against the metal. She didn't look around. He was laughing. The dogs disappeared. The catch flicked open and she stepped through the gate and onto the road. She didn't know which way to go. She turned left and didn't look back.

She carried the photographs in her hand and, after she had been walking for a time, began to tear them into tiny unrecognisable pieces and drop them in the grass at the side of the road. She skipped one in the pile and when all the others were gone she looked at it again. It was blurred and its colours seemed to have run as if it had been dipped in something. She could make out the shape of her own body, her skin shaded with blue and red. There was no one else in the photo, just her, and no one would have known it was her. She stared at the image then pushed it to the bottom of her bag.

She walked and walked until she felt sick and had to lurch off the road into the grass and hang her head ready to vomit. Nothing came out and after a while she continued walking on shaking legs. She realised she had left her shoes behind.

She sweltered under the sun and she could smell the sweat rising on her skin. She needed another drink.

She came to a house. Its front door was open but it looked deserted. She sat in the shade of a tree and rested and watched the house. The gate was open. A tap dripped in the shade of an old fence. She ventured into the yard and stopped at the tap and drank deeply; the water cool from the stiff metal vein of the pipe. She splashed water across her forehead and rubbed grimy marks from her arms. She walked back to the road. No one had come out or said anything. Just as well, she thought.

It felt late; past nine at least. She remembered she was supposed to be working in the shop. She began to run. Her father would kill her.

Susan drove all night. Adrenalin kept her awake. She was aware of every movement she made, every small decision. She had slipped out of the sleeping city like something that barely belonged there. She had seen herself reflected in water left behind by the summer storm she had pursued along the coast. She had had bad moments where she had just wanted to stop and go to sleep in a quiet bed. She had imagined the car floating into an oncoming truck and no time to say goodbye to anyone. She had remembered snatches of conver-

sation which made her skin burn, *You're so full of shit, so full
of pain and you don't even know it.* The words flowing gently
from his mouth. Blood through honey.

The sun rose and things began to look better. Her city street,
of children glimpsed through frames of warm yellow, of the
smell of dinners cooking, seemed like a dream left behind and
forgotten somewhere in the dark sprawl of unlit country
between. She was near the coast, and across the sea the air
was as clear as glass. She wound down the window and let
the wind dig around and catch in her dress. A sign appeared
at the side of the road.

Greenhill, it pointed; via Pilbeam. She was surprised to be
so close, so soon; her journey already over.

She turned off the highway and onto the narrower road. A
workman stopped her, stared at her for a while, then waved
her on through a section of road which coated the car with
fine white dust like flour.

The road weaved and wandered until it straightened into
the main street of Pilbeam. It was quiet. Dew still sparkled
on the grass where shade lay. Susan parked near the kiosk.
She stretched and her ears hummed in the vacuum of sound.
Stiffly, she pulled herself from the car and walked across the
grass to the river where the water slapped against the black
rocks of the breakwater. She stood and watched the water and
breathed in the salt air. Carloads of surfers drove past, staring
one-eyed out to sea in search of clean saltwater curls. She
ignored them. Once, it had been different. She and her friends
had written wrenching love letters to imaginary men and,
giggling, flung them into the sea in bottles, too scared to sign
their names. She smiled as she remembered.

There were things floating around here she didn't care to
remember. Pilbeam was so close to Greenhill yet it had seemed
like another world; light and sweet, somewhere to slip and
slide in and out of love, somewhere to imagine the rest of
your life.

She sat on the grass watching the river and listening to the surf. The sound made her head droop. Her head fell back onto the grass and she dozed. When she woke the day was older and hotter and she itched and her clothes were stuck to her skin. She needed a shower and food but there was something else she had to do first.

She walked back to the car and drove into Greenhill.

There were only a few people about. Shopkeepers were opening their shops. She drove past a grocery store, its lights flashing blindly in the daylight like a tiny Las Vegas. Advertising everything. She saw a young man with a large head standing with the shopkeeper and talking about something he held in his hands. The young man turned his head and watched her car roll down the street. She turned away but had already seen him wave to her. She pretended she hadn't and wondered if she had ever known him.

She turned up a street and followed it until she could see the buildings of the hospital. She parked the car and walked through the main entrance and down a long green hall until she found a nurse's station. She asked directions to his bed. The nurse looked her over. 'It's not visiting hours yet,' she said, pointing down the hall. 'Five-A,' she said, 'Be quick.'

Susan chewed her lip. Her foot was still sore from driving and she limped slightly, favouring her left until she reached the ward. Nurses bustled about and smiled at her. Old men lay on white sheets in chrome beds. The place smelled of antiseptic and she could see herself in the tiles on the floor. She turned a corner and saw him. Windows cut squares of brilliant blue from the walls. Light flooded the bed he was in, as if someone had forgotten him there, lying in the sun. She looked around, the old man opposite was watching her with unblinking eyes as if he knew everything about her and how long it had been since she had last visited.

She pulled the curtain across the window.

'Don't do that dear, he gets upset,' chimed a nurse, and he was already moving about, his arm pumping up and down with a fistful of sheet. She pulled the curtain back and he lay still again. She touched his leg and it was smooth and cool. She leant over him and whispered into his ear, 'Grandad, Grandad.'

The nurse stood beside the bed.

'He's a bit mixed up. He's much more active at night. He tries to get out of bed and has conversations with all sorts of people. He sleeps most of the day. Talk to him, dear. Hold his hand, he likes that.'

'Thank you.'

The nurse walked away.

Nothing but his chest moved; rising and falling, his gossamer breath parting his lips with a wet pop. His pyjama top was open and she could see how much weight he had lost—where muscle and flesh had once clung—since she had last seen him. She could see the scar of his war wound. It looked as if a fingerless doctor had once tried to fit some gruesome object *into* his body instead of taking something out. The scar had always made her skin creep. He turned onto his side and his penis, with its adornment of tubing and tape, sat exposed. She stared at it and then realised she was staring and blushed vividly. She looked at his face until he moved again.

Even though he was like this, or maybe because he was, she was glad she had seen him once more. She held his hand.

She looked over at the table beside him and was surprised to see a photograph in a frame, propped against a water jug. It was her, aged ten or eleven, standing in his garden, and at her side, Cliff, his arm snaking around her waist.

Sometimes I can see the shape of a man sitting out on the verandah behind the damn pebbled glass. He sits there all day and doesn't move at all, just sits there looking out. Sometimes I can smell him. He smells of split logs, smoke and dew. Sometimes he whistles.

I try to move, even an eyelid, but my head is a three-ring circus and the ringmaster is running through the bush blind drunk.

And can you blame him, cobber?

And sometimes I can feel the sun turn the sky over the ocean a deep plum, the earth revolving around my still centre. Aching bones. I remember air—fresh and clean—and the wind blowing as the light faded. I remember the time of the day when it would come as no surprise if someone long gone walked up and tapped you on the shoulder.

In the centre of Greenhill, in what should have been a cool place but wasn't, Cliff sweated in a pit under the body of a rusted ute. His arms were outstretched, feeling with his fingertips for something just out of sight and coated with mud and grease. His glasses were fogging so he closed his eyes. He wanted to stop; to get out. He heard footsteps. When he worked down here he kept the keys to the car in his pocket. He always pictured some idiot starting the car and driving off with his arms entwined amongst metal and hosing, pinned to the road by the solid mass of the car, his cheek burnt by exhaust, arms and then head chewed into the cylinder and burnt, the crack of the spark plug reflected in his glasses before they melted.

He felt for the keys in his pocket and relaxed as his hand curled around them. He reached for the part again, found it, unscrewed it, pulled it out, wiped it against his overalls and put it back. Hardly worth the bother, he thought. The car was shit. He bled the old oil and sat and watched it flow from the sump. He rested his aching back against the concrete wall. Metal dust gleamed in the light. He picked at his fingernails and the creases in his hands which held lines of oil and dirt like tattoos.

He heard voices, more footsteps. Someone was arguing with Davo. He could hear two voices getting louder, swimming around out there waiting to bite. He guessed it would be him who was bitten and his guess was right. They came into the garage and Davo called to him and he sighed and climbed out of the pit. There was a fat bloke with Davo and he was pissed off, his face twisted and red. Cliff heard words directed at him which he turned over and considered. Pig. Expensive. Incompetent. Damage. Money. It wasn't a pretty picture. He lit a cigarette. He knew that would probably annoy them. Davo leaned against the wall and pulled out his asthma puffer and sucked hard on it until the veins in his face glowed red. Cliff was tired of the shouting. It wasn't his fault and it wasn't that bad. The fat guy had money to burn. No, he didn't feel a bit sorry. He wondered why he was such a fuckhead, why there were so many fuckheads around lately. There were more and more all the time. His mind drifted and he wasn't listening any more. He was thinking of the girl. He smiled; he'd forgotten where he was and he smiled at that as well. He leaned against the wall, smoking his cigarette. 'I'll sue, you dozy prick!' he heard the fat guy say. Cliff turned back into the garage and told him to fuck himself, just loud enough for him to hear, just soft enough so he could deny it. The man said nothing for a while then pulled a mobile phone from his pocket and started jabbing at it.

Cliff cleaned his hands over the sink and disappeared out the back door into the sunshine. Davo followed him and his voice was tight and hoarse.

'You're this close mate!' He sounded like he meant it.

'Was it something we did?'

'No,' said Cliff. 'Not us.'

Cliff had worked at the garage for a long time and made Davo money so Davo took his word for it. Cliff imagined losing his job and the thought made no impression either way. No fear or dread. Nothing.

He walked away from the garage. It felt like being let out of school before the bell. He walked along the street and looked at the ground and noticed the smallness of things down there. It was Friday afternoon on a stinking day in the country; there was only one place to go.

On the way there he stepped into the cool brick shade of the post office and took a key from his pocket and opened the lock of a post office box with it. Number sixty-three. Inside was a card to collect a parcel from the counter. A cool blast of air flowed from the open box and Cliff bent and let it dry the sweat from his face. Someone came up the stairs behind him and he flicked the little door shut. He stepped into the post office and stood in the queue, then handed the man the card and waited. After a while the man reappeared with the parcel and Cliff took it from him and turned and walked back out onto the street and squeezed his eyes shut against the glare.

Main Street.

Two blocks held the shops of Greenhill. Most of the buildings were wooden and sported fading coats of paint and dust.

Cliff walked past empty shopfronts with long unwashed windows. Kids were throwing stones around. He picked up a stone with his free hand and flung it at a cat lying in the sun. He missed. The kids cried out delightedly and copied him and soon stones were skimming close to windows as the cat escaped up the side of the building along pipes and sills. There was a crash and the tinkling of glass. The kids howled and scattered and Cliff, laughing, ran too.

On the balcony of the hotel across the street, a tenant watched the window break, watched Cliff run and the cat return to its spot in the sun. Then his head sank to his chest and he slept once more.

The sun burned Cliff's back and dried his mouth. He stared at the parcel he held. There were three hotels on the street arranged in a rough triangle. He picked the one which would be shaded later on. Its green tiles still winked in the sun. The glass panes in the door were frosted and crossed by a bar of bright chrome. He pushed against the bar and stepped inside and his eyes strained and were useless for a moment in the gloom. A dozen pairs of eyes shook him down at the door then turned away. He knew without having to look that there were half a dozen old codgers sitting on stools near the window on his left, cigarettes glowing in their mouths. He could hear them coughing and hawking. They knew him and used to know his father and his grandfather. He had heard all their stories.

The hotel was cheap and worn and grog did most of the talking. A few men sat alone, scanning newspapers with shaky hands or staring out into the street.

Cliff settled onto a stool and rested his feet on the steel ashtray sitting on the floor. He was not in the mood to talk or listen. He wanted to drink. He wanted to hear a joke he hadn't heard before. He lit a cigarette, closed his eyes, stretched his hand across his forehead and rubbed his skull through the flesh, pushing the blood around like water in a sponge. His head ached from petrol fumes and heat. The barman poured him a beer and set it before him; a tall cone of gold bleeding condensation onto the counter. He drank. It was like pouring water straight into your lungs; maybe like drowning.

He drank faster than he could think.

'Hot enough for ya?'
'Yep.'
'Any plans for the weekend?'
'Nup.'

The barman worked silently, wiping the broad wooden bar, stopping here and there like a slow bee. He poured beer after beer for the men perched around the high tables.

Cliff sat and drank for hours. The paper in his pocket turned to metal. He watched the television flickering in the

18

corner and smoked cigarette after cigarette. He watched fascinated as a crippled man walked across the floor; the lopsided roll of his gait like a buckled wheel. He peeled his bony arse off the stool and followed the man to the toilet. He was interested to see how he went, how he held himself up. Cliff tried to look but the man eyed him viciously and Cliff gave up and went back to the bar.

He counted the change in his pocket and eyed the rows of honey-coloured bottles on the shelves. He ordered whisky and swallowed it clean and ordered another and went and sat near the window looking out at the street and the people moving along it. Their faces seemed familiar and interesting. Things began to float and then he began to float. He could feel pressure in his head as if something was trying to get out. More people came through the doors. Fat-bellied bastards. He turned and watched them. In from hard work. Too many. He didn't want to run into anyone from the waterhole.

He staggered into the street which was glowing now in the soft afternoon light. He walked past blasted neon, clapped-out fluorescent, rubbish in the gutter. Warm brown puddles in the street like brown open mouths. Panting dogs ran loose, circulating around the block, testing the air with wet noses and pink tongues, stopping only to fight or piss against telegraph poles.

Details filtered through to him and were then forgotten. People appeared: mottle-faced and leering, picking their noses with thick red fingers and yelling at him from doorways, vanishing back into them as he passed. The town had changed, it wasn't the same any more. Home. There was nowhere else to go. There was a plantation of marijuana in the bush behind his house. It was a magnet to the people in town who knew about it. Sometimes he would come home and they would have started without him, the house sometimes looking like it was on fire. He didn't care. He had come home once and found kids lying on the beds and on the lounge like a brood of runty gnomes, all stoned, the house in a greater mess than he had ever seen.

He walked down the lane behind the shops toward the bridge. He saw the pet shop still open. He hadn't been there for months. He decided to buy a fish for his tank. It'll be someone to talk to on the way home, he thought. Yep, he'd give the fish an earful, see what the fish had to say about it all. Fuck it, he'd get two, have twice the conversation.

He peered at the watch floating along his arm. It was a few minutes to five. Loads of time. The fish shop was only a minute away and he ran, throwing his long legs in front of him. He ran around the corner and frightened an old lady half to death, twirling around and just grazing her, impressing himself with the fine control he had over his body. He burst through the shop door. The few people there stared at his greasy overalls and big black boots and wild hair. He ignored them, easily. The fish were the things. He bent and squinted into the tanks, trying to focus his eyes but the fish seemed to be swimming out of their tanks, right around his head.

'What have you got now? Flying fish?' he said to no one in particular.

'Not today,' said a voice beside him. 'Can I help you with anything?'

He looked up and his balls froze. Sweat sprouted everywhere.

It was her. It was the pale girl.

'Um, ah, yes please. Could I have one of those and one of those?' He jabbed somewhere with his finger.

'Those ones?'

'Yeah.'

'How many?'

'Um . . . three. No, four.'

He looked around. He didn't want to look at her. He wondered if she had seen him at the waterhole. She must have. The owner of the shop was staring at him. He was a surly-looking bugger, Cliff thought. Roy someone. He had a big lump on the side of his neck. He turned back and glued his eyes somewhere up behind her, high up on the wall.

'Any one in particular?'

'No.'

She reached in to catch the fish. He watched her. He felt sick. A thick silver bangle slid down her arm. There was a leather band around her wrist but no watch. She looked different this close. He noticed a curve like a shadow beside her mouth, its angle mimicking the tilt of her lips. She pulled hair out of her eyes and chased fish with the net. She seemed to be smiling.

His chest still heaved from the run. He stood with his hands on his hips. She gave him the bag of fish, said something he didn't catch, then disappeared through a door at the back of the shop and did not return. He took the fish to the counter and paid Roy and walked out of the shop. He had no money left.

It was cool outside, and darker. He crossed the street and looked back at the shop and the empty windows of the flat above it. He was tired. He scratched his nose with his arm, gently, so it wouldn't start bleeding. He knew what he must look like, smell like. He knew women wanted men to smell nice. If you didn't smell nice you could forget it. It was that simple, he knew it was; all the other stuff was garbage. You just had to be clean. And funny. Clean and funny. Clean and funny. He repeated the words to himself as he shambled along the street; then over the bridge to the other side of the river.

Safe.

He didn't talk to the fish as he had planned; he didn't even look at them through the clear plastic. He hoped no one was in his house.

After Cliff left, Roy ushered out the last customer and locked the door with a fat black padlock. He turned, expected to see his daughter but she wasn't there. He listened and heard the boards creak above his head. He swore and began to clean up the shop.

Jade watched Cliff walk away. When he looked up at the window she stepped back into the darkness. She leant from the window as he continued along the street. She didn't know why she watched him go; something about him. She turned and went back downstairs to her father. She could hear him moving around, doing things with twice as much noise as he needed to; the way he did when something annoyed him. She was sick of that. Sick of the shop. Sick of his music. She stayed out for days just to spite him but she was sick of that too. God knew she was.

She couldn't look him in the eye any more. It wasn't working. She had known all along it wouldn't and she had told him. They barely knew each other.

Some mornings he would rest his wet head on hers as she sat at the table eating breakfast. He said he loved the warm sweet smell of her. She would bend away from him. He could be so charming, fresh from the shower. Sometimes she laughed at his jokes despite herself. She would sit on the step and listen to his stories of Asia. He needed to be quite drunk to talk but even when he was falling down he never mentioned her mother. All the stories yet he never told her the things she needed to know. If she asked him straight he would clam up, or disappear. She had found him asleep in the front yard some mornings and had had to open the shop herself.

'Why did Mum go?' she had asked him.

'Where is she now?'

No use of course.

She went into her room and changed, throwing her dirty clothes onto a pile behind the door. She had to get out.

Roy mopped the floor. Jade came down the stairs. He could see her mother in the way she moved; never his own hard shape and he was glad of that.

'Go put on a dress,' he said. 'We can go somewhere nice. Have something to eat.'

She said nothing so he tried again.

'Why don't you clean yourself up a bit and we can go?'

Nothing again. She was glaring at him. He snapped and shouted at her.

'What's the matter now?'

'Nothing.'

'What did I say?'

'Nothing. See you later.'

She slipped out the door into the night.

Roy mopped the floor, concentrating on the feel of the wooden handle in his hands, breathing slowly. Slow even strokes over the floor until it was clean.

Cliff opened his eyes and blinked. His head throbbed. It was daylight again and he could hear the television talking to itself. He pulled himself up and turned it off. It was very quiet without it. He ached all over. He held his head in his hands for a few minutes. Behind his eyelids he saw a giant woman with his mother's eyes standing over him, shouting, her finger wagging.

Just a dream, he thought, I don't remember that.

He opened his eyes and the image was gone.

He stood unsteadily with his head lowered and eyes closed again against the light. He took two steps to the window and supported himself on the lintel with one hand and pulled down his zip with the other and pissed gold into the garden.

When he was ready to move again he went to the bathroom and held his head under the shower, turned on the cold tap, and held his breath as the water hit him. He drank some. He went into the kitchen, opened the fridge and peered inside. There was beer and milk and things in plastic bags. He picked up a bottle of beer and unscrewed the top and drank, swilling it around in his mouth. The bubbles tickled him and he sneezed. His nose kicked in and he could smell smoke in his clothes. Curly came in and sniffed him. Cliff poured the rest of the beer into Curly's bowl and Curly lapped it up.

'Morning, mate.'

He opened another beer and walked back to the bathroom and had a shower. The beer sat where the soap usually did. His body drank in the heat like a stone. He brushed his teeth, stuck his glasses under the tap and brushed them too. He shaved; trying not to look at himself in the mirror. As usual, shaving gave him a rash and he poured aftershave onto his hand and splashed it on his face where it burnt and stung. He swore. He was awake.

He walked down the hall. There was a bag of fish sitting on top of the fish tank. They looked like goldfish. They were. Coldwater fish. His tank was tropical. They looked dead.

He upended the bag into the tank and watched the other fish tear them apart until there was nothing left but a smoky trail of blood and delicate pieces of fin fluttering down like tiny watery butterflies.

'Dickhead,' he said.

He left the tank and wandered around the house. He had nothing on and dried himself in the breeze like a piece of washing. His stomach growled and he searched the fridge and cupboards again for something to eat. He scratched the thick scrub of hair on his chest. He found his cigarettes. There was nothing in the kitchen but tea so he boiled water and made a pot and drank it white and sweet on the step. He looked out at the fine blue morning and savoured the air in his lungs, slipping across his skin. He lit a cigarette. The nicotine banged into his blood and made his hand tremble. He drained the mug of tea and refilled it from the pot. He opened another bottle of beer and sucked on it. He sat for an hour on the step, naked still. He sipped the tea and the beer alternately and listened to things. He spotted the dark specks of ships as they steamed by. The sea looked peaceful from this distance but he knew there was a big swell running; he could just see the white tip on the crest of each wave, rolling along.

Daniel found his way. He drove down streets he knew. Greenhill. Back again. He recognised houses and watched uniformed children walking near a school. He stopped and knocked on a few doors. He watched himself do it. He wondered what he was doing and why he was doing it. People he spoke to looked at him strangely and distrustfully. He didn't blame them. When he looked in the mirror in the morning he didn't trust himself. He searched their faces, trying to see something he recognised, or looking to see whether they were as amazed at what came out of his mouth as he was.

He saw a house he knew. It stood out from the others in the street because the front yard overflowed with trees and shrubs. The house hid behind them. A cat perched on the step in the sun with half-closed eyes. The house seemed the same except the trees were much bigger than he remembered and there was a little garden bed under the front windows filled with struggling flowers.

He stopped the car in front of the house and crossed to the gate and pushed against it. It squealed. Nervous, he walked down the path. He had a dreamy, jumpy kind of feeling in his stomach and his tongue was fat in his mouth.

The cat sprang out of the way as he walked up the stairs and before he had even knocked the door was opened by a little white-haired lady, an antique, immaculately dressed and smiling at him.

'Hello,' he said, 'I used to live here.'

She won't let me in, he thought, but she did.

Her face wrinkled and she offered him tea.

He said, 'Yes, that would be nice.' So they sat and sipped tea from fine white china and nibbled biscuits.

'Where are your people now, dear?' she asked.

'They moved to the city,' he said.

He told her his memories of the house and she listened and nodded. He couldn't remember much. He looked at her pictures around the room and assumed the man was her husband and he was dead. There were other pictures: herself with her husband, other men. He was curious. She saw where his eyes wandered but only smiled at him primly. He wondered whether she had always been so polite, and what she had talked about with these men after tea: after dark.

The house had been painted but not recently. It was brighter, cleaner, and smelled of old furniture.

Her trust made him unbearably sad. He left. She seemed sad to see him go.

He drove around. He didn't want to talk to anyone. He stopped in the main street and bought fried chicken and chips from a milk bar and walked over to the park to eat. He lay on the grass under a tree. Kids chased each other and parents chased them. The tree seemed to be floating just above him. His eye traced the blue inlets of sky. The tree swayed and dropped leaves. An ant crawled over his hand.

The river rolled by. The long stringy heart of Greenhill. The town followed a sweeping bend in the river. The land rose on either side to form a valley. Trees clung to the high places and hid cliffs and waterfalls.

Daniel watched slicks of oil float by. Old docks rotting and waiting for a flood to send them out to sea. Vines covered the banks and bees scraped their purple flowers clean. He imagined crabs as big as hubcaps on the riverbed, feeding on drowned cats. Fish with whiskers like the tails of mice, trawling through the mud, somewhow avoiding broken glass, rusted junk.

He was ready to go. He tried to think of someone he

wanted to see again before he left. If he was about to die, shouldn't there be someone he wanted to see? He thought of a few teachers and dismissed them; he doubted they wanted to see *him* again. Not even any relatives left here. A name sprang into his head like a shout. Of course.

He stood up and stretched and yawned and hurried to the car. His hand burnt and he could see a red lump. Bloody ant. He felt dizzy and wondered if he was allergic.

He backed out into the street and drove towards the bridge. The road baked in the sun. Cars weaved around the street like drunks dodging potholes. The bridge clanked as he drove over it. He drove past the railway station and then across the flats and up the gentle slope of the valley. The road twisted through trees and barrelled through paddocks filled with cattle who lifted their heads and watched him as he passed. He waved to them. He rounded a bend and nearly turned around when he saw the house and the fig tree which towered beside it. The boards of the house were scaly with old paint, warped and split.

Lousy mongrel bastard, he thought. Do it.

The door was open and a dog stood in the doorway and watched him get out of the car and walk up the steps.

Curly!

He reached down and scratched the dog's head.

He heard a noise from inside the house and looked up. What struck him first was the familiar shape of him. He was older, heavier; a face like a building, solid, bottom lip like a step; a gap between his teeth he could spit through. He knew him, knew the eyes and the hair. Each looked at the other and then each said the other's name in the same second.

'Cliff.'

'Daniel!'

Both were as surprised as the other and both hid their pleasure with a casual greeting.

'How are you, you ugly bastard?'

'Good. How are *you*, you dumb cocknocker?'

'Fine. Dandy.'

'What are you doing here?'

'Do you want to buy some aluminium siding?'

'Shit!'

They had been best friends at school. They shook hands. It seemed like the right thing to do.

'Come in. Take your fuckin' tie off! Have a beer!'

Daniel followed Cliff through the house and into the kitchen. Cliff was as tall and loose as he remembered. He wore jeans with their arse and knees out and a white T-shirt. Cliff slapped him on the back—so hard it stung—and said 'shit' again. He plucked two beers from the fridge and handed one to Daniel with a grin like it was the key to a fast car. Daniel watched him, noticed the grime on his hands, and was unsure what to say next.

'I . . . ahhhh.'

Cliff's face split in a goofy grin. His head lifted as if he were about to sneeze; then he laughed, a hoot that Daniel had never forgotten.

He hadn't changed at all.

In school he had always been quiet, but his laugh was enough to set off whole classes, teachers included.

'What's so funny?' asked Daniel.

'I dunno.' Cliff laughed some more.

Questions waited or went unspoken and it was just like it had been before.

They drank the beer and Cliff went to the fridge and rummaged inside it and then swore.

'I've run out of bloody beer! Can you believe it? On a day like today. You don't have to be anywhere do ya?'

Daniel could have said yes, or, don't worry about it, and he nearly did.

'No,' he said.

'Come on, we'll go down and get some.'

He followed Cliff back down the long central hall of the house. There were closed doors on each side. He had never been inside Cliff's house before. None of his friends had.

'Where are your grandparents?'

'My grandma's dead, my grandad's nearly dead.'

Cliff walked into a room and rummaged around looking for something. Daniel followed him. The walls were covered in pictures painted directly onto the boards. There was painting after painting of naked women, monsters, dragons, strange animals in lurid yellows, purples, greens, reds and blues like stained glass. Dominating one wall was a painting of a man with skin the colour of blood. Daniel ran his hand over a section of the wall and felt the tiny ridges of paint. The pictures were interspersed with spray-can tags. Cans of paint and brushes littered the ground. Beer bottles, cigarette packets, overflowing ashtrays, scraps of food and rubbish, photographs, were strewn across the room.

Cliff found his keys, straightened, and saw Daniel looking at the walls.

'They're amazing,' said Daniel finally. 'I didn't know you could paint!'

'I can't. It's just mucking around, copying things. Come on, let's go.'

'Yeah, okay.' Daniel shook his head and smiled.

They climbed into Cliff's car: an old wreck of a Ford with piebald patches of bodywork. Curly jumped in as well and sat panting on the back seat. They took off in a spray of dust and smoke and wound back down the road that Daniel had just driven up. Something was on the wet edge of Daniel's tongue but whatever it was stayed there.

Cliff drove to the nearest hotel and bought a carton of beer from its bottle shop. He threw it on the back seat.

'Now we're set,' he said.

Cliff worked the old car along the road with nonchalant skill and haphazard road manners. He indicated points of interest in the town with his hand as they sped through it; things that had changed, things that were the same. His arm hung from the car like a rudder. His cigarette glowed and showered sparks. He didn't bring his arm in to change gear but left the wheel free, meshing the gears of the wheezing engine, giving it all the help he could and swearing softly at it under his breath.

Daniel had never known anyone else like Cliff.

The roar of the car cut any conversation. The sticky air rushed past their ears. The day was fading and Daniel noticed storm clouds brewing in the sky. Cliff sucked on his cigarette then lit another from it and offered one to Daniel. Cliff turned on the radio and the car floated through the corners as it sped up. Cliff turned up the volume.

'Only thing in here that works properly!' he shouted.

They were taking the long way back to the house. Cliff turned off the road onto a dirt track. The car fishtailed over crests, and trees on either side of the road began to meet overhead. The road was rough; rocks the size of potatoes banged against the bottom of the car and bounced off into the scrub. Clouds blocked the last light of the sun.

'Looks like it's going to rain,' Daniel shouted.

'Yep. It's gunna piss down in a minute. I'll see if I can beat it.'

Cliff accelerated and used both his hands to steer. The track climbed upwards.

'Nearly there,' said Cliff cheerfully.

The house loomed as rain fell and lightning flashed. Cliff steered the car directly to the front steps and wound up his window. Daniel did the same and retrieved the beer from the back seat and followed Cliff up the stairs to the verandah. Blue paint fell from the railing where he touched it and clung to his hand. They turned around and stood, panting, sipping beer between breaths.

'You can see the ocean from here,' Cliff said. 'Sometimes when it's really quiet you can hear it as well.'

They sat down on the wooden boards of the verandah and watched the storm break overhead. Rain lashed the car and sent steam curling up from the bonnet. Lightning lit the countryside and bounced off the river like quicksilver. The lights of Greenhill winked on and off through the rain. Daniel imagined people caught out, dressed up for the evening, wet and laughing. He imagined people he knew, asleep or listening to rain somewhere else; softer than this, trickling down gutters.

Trees bent and roared in the wind and somewhere a sheet of metal began to flap and bang. Cliff was quiet, unconcerned; his face darkened by shadow, staring forward. As soon as it had started the heavy rain stopped and was replaced by rain from a gentler cloud. In the distance lightning continued to flash and in the flickering light Daniel saw the white crescent of the beach—the white surf—before darkness enveloped it.

'Come on in,' Cliff said.

Daniel followed him into the straight and solid spaces of the house. A musty smell he hadn't noticed before crept up from the floor, the furniture. Cliff snapped on a light and it blazed for a moment and then faded to an orange ember. He threw his keys onto a table and bent and switched on a lamp sitting on the floor. Daniel noticed the walls shining in the light. They were wet and cool to the touch as though a reservoir was concealed at the heart of the house. Water ran in tiny streams from two stained areas of the ceiling. He noticed buckets, pots and pans scattered on the floor catching drips. There was a large black lounge, stereo, and television. A fish tank stood against a wall. He could see the fish circulating like clockwork toys. Cobwebs hung decoratively from the ceiling.

'The roof needs fixing,' said Cliff.

'Yeah.'

Cliff went to the table and picked up a metal container and unscrewed its lid. He took out a joint like a finger and offered it to Daniel.

'I've got a few plants in the scrub,' said Cliff.

They sat on the lumpy foam of the couch and puffed on the joint between mouthfuls of beer. Cliff put music on and turned the volume up. The sound made Daniel's heart beat faster. They had always liked the same music. It took on colours that seeped and swirled across the room.

'Music keeps me sane,' said Cliff.

'Yeah,' said Daniel. He couldn't think of anything else to say.

They sat and some of the heat of the day returned in the wake of the storm. Cliff stood and took off his shirt. His back was tattooed with a winged beast and a skull with snakes through its eyes. On his shoulder and arm was a woman; her hair trailed like a green stain down his arm to his elbow. Her face was coloured with war paint. They moved over his skin and Daniel tried to avoid looking at them. He felt very sleepy.

Cliff was full of surprises.

They looked at each other and laughed at nothing as the drug climbed cables and sat perched somewhere inside their heads. Daniel sat screwed into his chair for what seemed like hours. Cliff turned down the music to a whisper and went and sat outside. Daniel, with a lot of effort, followed. The sweet scent of the drug lingered, mingling with the fresh timber smell of the wet trees. To their left a long ridge wound its way up from the coast and disappeared in the dark to the west. It was steep, notched with cliffs and covered with trees which swayed in the washed air. Bats flew overhead, silent on their wings of stretched skin. Daniel could hear them squabbling and screaming. He tried to imagine walking up into the scrub but the thought was too much and he moved his eyes down to his hands and studied them.

The lighthouse appeared like another star, low in the sky.

Cliff began to talk. Daniel heard his voice clearly even though it was soft and husky.

'When this place was first settled,' Cliff said, 'a convict escaped from a jail down south and came up here. He murdered someone. He was trying to get as far away as he could so they wouldn't bother coming to catch him. He came up here and lived up in the bush behind us.'

He waved his hand.

'Did I ever tell you this story?'

'No.'

'You can still see where his shack was if you know where to look. He stayed there for years, living off the land, only coming into town now and then and never telling anyone anything about himself. For a long time he did this until he got careless and went into town more often to drink. He was tattooed so he stood out. There was a new copper in town and he heard about this bloke from the bush and tried to find out who he was. It took him a while but he finally figured it out. He and some troopers went to catch him. They hadn't ever forgotten about him. Someone tipped off the convict and he walked up into the hills to lie low. The captain got a black tracker who tracked him through the bush until they came to an old fig. They couldn't see him but the black said he was there. They searched everywhere until they found a gap in the tree. He was inside the tree—hiding. They ordered him out but he wouldn't come, so they lit a fire in front of the hole. But he still didn't come out. They could hear him inside, swearing and carrying on. They made the fire bigger until they couldn't hear anything. He was dead.'

Daniel looked at Cliff and noticed his glasses seemed to be wired together.

'The poor bugger doesn't rest in peace. You can still hear

him when it's quiet, calling out to the captain, looking for him. Some people have seen him walking through the bush at night with a lantern, swinging it from side to side so people will stay out of his way. They say if you get too close and he lifts his hat and you look into his eyes you'll drop dead of fright.'

The hair on Daniel's neck prickled.

Cliff turned and grinned at Daniel and started to laugh and the laugh echoed and fed on itself until Cliff sat wheezing and holding his belly.

'Should have seen your face!'

'You bastard! You're still the same!'

They sat until Cliff's giggling subsided. He had always laughed long and hard at his own jokes.

Cliff spoke again. 'I've been having a dream,' he said. 'I'm flying around outside and something's chasing me, some kind of spike, about a foot round. I can hear it humming and there's nothing I can do, it's too fast. It slides into me and I watch it go in. But no blood comes out, only smoke. Then I wake up. What do you reckon?'

Daniel said nothing. His mouth was dry, oily currents in his head sucked away anything coherent. He looked at Cliff as he answered him.

'I think you need a holiday.'

Cliff laughed again. He thought it was nearly as funny as his own joke.

'You're probably right,' he said at last. 'What are you doing back here anyway?'

'It's a long story.'

'Tomorrow?'

'Yep.'

Daniel turned his head. Cliff's tattoo writhed on his arm and his glasses hid his eyes. It had always been hard for him to understand Cliff, how his mind worked. He pictured his brain as clusters of thick and soft wire, slipping and sliding against each other; white sparks of short circuits, blue smoke erupting from his ears like a cartoon character.

He felt himself tiring. He had had vague thoughts of waiting for the sun to rise over the ocean, but the night seemed to have gone on for long enough. His eyelids dropped. He was asleep when Cliff picked him up and carried him to the lounge and set him down gently upon it.

Cliff kept on drinking. He wasn't tired. The bottle felt comfortable in his hand. He rubbed it across his forehead and felt its coolness bite into his brow. He held up his finger and measured the distance between the dark crown of the fig tree and the bright star above it. He lifted his glasses and the star disappeared into the black flume of space. He lowered them and waited until the earth had moved and the star had dropped behind the topmost leaves on the topmost branches. He went to his room and lay on his bed. He took off his glasses and fell asleep after running his eyes along the blurred edges of the room.

The house was built so that breeze drifted through it like music.

Sometime before morning Daniel woke to the sound of a young child running across the roof. It was a long time before the child grew fur and claws and his open face transformed into the wide-eyed gaze of a possum.

Roy fried a sausage, a rasher of bacon and an egg and then ate in silence. When he had finished he stepped outside. His neighbour who lived over one of the other shops came out into his yard with rubbish in his hands. Roy raised his hand to hail him but the shout stopped dry in his throat. The neighbour dropped the rubbish in his bin and then walked back inside without raising his head. Roy waited and then went back into his flat. It was quiet inside. He hovered outside Jade's door. He knocked. No answer. He opened the door. She was not in her bed.

He stood and looked around the room. Her suitcase still wasn't completely empty. It lay half under the bed. Her dressing-table was covered in jewellery, bottles of cream, perfume, makeup. Her mirror swam under clothes. He held his head and rubbed his fingers over his skull. He had no language to describe the empty room. He bent and picked up an armful of her clothes from the floor, pressed them to his face like flowers, held them, and wet them with tears.

The beach

Michael smelled the air. Miles away, rain. Trees flowering across the range: white and pale orange.

He looked back from where he had walked. The plains were black and still. He bent, coughed savagely, then straightened. He took a last look before sleep, then wrapped himself in the blanket he carried on his back. He had not spoken to another person for months. He had slept beside the silent landscape of cotton, beneath grey and twisted trees, beside sweet water. He had listened to powerlines sing and watched willy-willys dance but people seemed not to see him; even though he walked straight through their land, across their borders. He had disappeared into heat haze and he had lost his voice. The day saved him from night. Soon he would see the ocean.

He smiled, lay down in the grass and curled up. It was cold in the hills and he lay as close to the fire glowing on the rock as his aching hands would let him. He held himself, touched his body with a gnarled and numb hand and disappeared inside his own shape. When he slept he saw his pursuer wake, smell the change as easily as he had, and follow.

The morning was a promise; as clear and blue as a dream. It stretched out to the horizon, cloudless; the welcoming blue of it an after-image that you could chase for hours. The sun shone like a beacon.

Daniel woke, looked around, and went back to sleep. He woke again later, the vague memory of a dream poised like a diver inside him. It was quiet except for the sound of birds whipping messages to each other outside. He lay listening for a while then wandered down the hall and found the bathroom. On the floor sat a mirror, one corner cracked like a spider's web; the shards held together with flaking yellow tape. It was bordered with mother-of-pearl. He pressed his finger against the razored edges and they moved against each other with a tiny scraping whisper. He looked at his finger and was surprised to see a bloodless track through the ridges and whorls of his fingerprint.

His head felt clearer than it had for a long time. He trod outside to the verandah and looked out across the valley. The air washed around his body and woke him. A cup of coffee and the day would be perfect, he thought.

The rest of his life seemed far away. There was nothing to trouble him. He noticed a little statue of a man holding the door open. A little oriental man. He seemed to be smiling. He was cold to the touch.

Cliff's cigarettes were lying on the boards. He took one and held it in his hand for a few minutes, then lit it, inhaled, and walked out onto the wet grass under the trees. He stepped into the sun and lifted his head and bathed his face in the warmth. Stars and pinwheels appeared before his eyes and as he chased them they vanished. Smoke crept into the corner of his eye and made tears run. He closed his eyes and waited for something to happen.

Nothing did. Then the smell of coffee rolled out the doorway. Cliff was up. Soon, he came out with a brimming cup and handed it to Daniel.

'Morning.'

'Morning.'

'It's a beautiful day,' said Daniel.

'Yeah. Not bad.'

'Not bad? How can it get any better than this?'

Cliff shrugged. 'I'm just used to it I suppose,' he said.

They sat and the sun peeled cooler air away from shade and shadow. The air around the house filled with a passing traffic of insects; their bony armour caught the sun and conjured tiny rainbows from it.

'Come on. We'll go for a swim to wake up.'

Daniel started. He had been far away, back in the city.

'What?'

Cliff went into the house and came back with two towels. A black felt hat had appeared on his head. It drooped over his face and Daniel chuckled at him.

'What's so funny?'

'Nothing, nothing.'

Cliff sprang on Daniel's back and he fell forward into the grass and ate some. Cliff whooped triumphantly. Daniel throught his back had been broken. He stood up and felt light-headed and thin. Cliff was already striding up the slope behind the house towards the bush. Daniel followed him gingerly.

At the base of the scrub Daniel stopped and looked up; standing there was like standing at the bottom of a huge green wave, whispering and rustling, about to break.

They slipped under the canopy and out of sight of the rest of the world. The light faded into a gloomy soup. Daniel followed Cliff along the slightest hint of a track, over huge buttressed roots and creeks swollen by the storm. Their feet sank in drifts of leaves. The temperature increased. Daniel could smell his body, could taste cigarette smoke in his mouth and lungs. He sweated until his body was as slick as the leaves around him. He could hear lizards rustling through the undergrowth as they walked past. He thought he knew the place Cliff was headed for, but he had never walked there from this direction. They had always reached it by crossing the railway line down near the road. He remembered walking along the tracks throwing rocks at each other, smoking cigarettes Cliff had stolen from somewhere, sitting in the dirt under the bridge and imagining girls from school naked and shameless.

The track steepened and Cliff began to wheeze and cough.

'Not as fit as we used to be hey?' he said to Daniel.

'Nowhere near.'

'My grandad used to spend hours and hours in here, day and night, just walking around.'

'At night?'

'Yeah. Used to scare the shit out of me with stories of things he'd seen.'

'Like what?'

'You know, ghosts and spirits and things.'

'Not real though?'

'Real enough.' Cliff grinned.

Daniel remembered Cliff's grandad telling them off for something; or sitting so still somewhere for so long they thought he must have died.

They reached the top of the hill and then began to descend. The scrub became thicker and thicker. The track disappeared and they walked over bare rock. They climbed over boulders and onto a broad platform. In front of them was a wide pool of water with a low waterfall at one end.

Cliff went to a rock which jutted out into the pool, took off all his clothes and jumped in, the sound echoing and reverberating like an explosion. Daniel, slowly, did the same. The water sucked the breath from his body. He laughed from the shock and thrashed his limbs to circulate his blood. He ducked his head and blocked out all sound except for the smooth hum of water rushing over rock. Something brushed against his foot and he yelped as he hit the surface and splashed toward the shore and scrambled out. His feet were numb. Cliff was laughing, sitting on a half-submerged rock.

'Did he get you?'

'Bastard, I hate eels.'

'I know!'

Daniel dried himself with the towel and lay down in the sun. Cliff heaved himself from the pool, sprayed Daniel with water from his hair and lay down on his towel and lit a cigarette. Daniel watched the smoke build in the still air and hang like a hazy double beside him.

'No one ever comes up here much,' said Cliff.

The smoke beside him moved and seemed to punctuate his words.

Daniel reached out for the cigarettes.

'Here you go,' said Cliff.

He knew he shouldn't but it didn't seem to matter as much any more. The smoke from the cigarette filled his lungs, cloaking his sight for a moment so it became as grainy as an old movie. His heart beat faster. Trees circled the pool; air and light wound around leaves and sent something more than magical slipping down branches and trunks to the forest floor.

Daniel thought he could probably lie there for the rest of his life.

I remember a girl handing me a flower as I walked through her pretty village. I dreamt of her much later; her face strained and hurt and collapsing in a flash of blood. In this way I carried home what I had seen and it was a long journey from France to Greenhill.

I killed my mate there. Did I say? Shot him clean through the throat as we fought side by side. It used to be an accident. I was only a boy. No one ever knew. People wondered, guessed, but no one knew what I felt and I never told a soul, not my wife, not even the other one.

I dug into his neck with my fingers with a wild idea that if I could find the bullet he would be saved.

Susan drove up the short driveway to the house and the wheels of the car spun in the wet grass. She braked, turned off the ignition, and wound down the window. The house looked even more run-down than she remembered. The yard was a mess; rusted machinery sat like islands in the long grass, weeds grew everywhere. She knew what she would see if she turned around: a green quilt of cane, black swell of headland, sea, the curve of the river. She got out of the car and walked up to the house. The ground, fed by a drainpipe from the roof, was sodden. She raised her arms for balance. She was used to concrete. The spongy lawn surprised her, tested her. She thought of moats and man-traps but the house looked too tired, too old for games. The door was open. She could see down the hall into the backyard. Two cars were parked at the side of the house. One, almost new, the other a near wreck. She called his name and her voice was hollow in the breeze. Maybe he's asleep, she thought. She called again, louder. Still no answer.

She stood on the bottom step, and then, slowly, walked up. Here, on the top step, and later in a chair on the verandah, Grandad would sit and pipe smoke his tobacco. She would hide among the bushes, listening to his small movements, his creaks, his sighs. Back then, she had thought she was so quiet, invisibly quiet; no possible way he could know she was there but then he would laugh and tell her to come out. She would sit like another old man beside him and pretend to see what it was that interested him out in the dark. He would coat her with the black of his eye and warm her heart.

She reached the door. The lock was gutted and useless and it was held open by a squat metal statue. She reached down and polished the Buddha's belly with her thumb. Grandad believed in a reservoir of luck; he became angry when unimportant things went his way. 'The tank's getting dry,' he would say.

She entered the hall and shook her head. She inspected the house with her hands on her hips, chewing her lip. It smelt like a smoking carriage on a train stuck on a siding with no air-conditioning. There was no one home and she was relieved.

The kitchen was lit by a field of glass. It hadn't changed; it was as if no time at all had passed. Gran's plates were stacked in the cabinet exactly as she remembered. The sink was full of dishes. A cardboard box of empty bottles sat near the back door. Flies buzzed around and landed to drink, up to their elbows in flat beer. Susan contemplated walking out the door and going home.

She looked out the window at the backyard. It was overgrown; the mulberry tree draped with a creeping vine. She remembered being stained with sweet juice, black and sticky on her skin. Gran's old washing machine squatted beside the garden shed, its metal pitted and rusted. Gran's arms feeding clothes through the wringer while she kept one eye on her grandchildren. Cool cement sinks. The coolest place to be in summer; she and Cliff splashing each other until Gran would send them spinning and squealing into the yard.

The kitchen table and the floor were smooth and worn. The same colour as if they were from the same tree. Old cooking smells lay under the surface of things. A spider crawled out of a cupboard, low slung and villainous. Susan picked up a can of spray and attacked. A scent of flowers filled the air. Air freshener. She laughed, then stopped. The spider twitched and died anyway.

So much time had slipped by.

She looked into the lounge and saw the pictures on the

walls. She had been apprehensive but now she began to worry. She remembered painting a picture at school when she was very little and showing her grandfather and he had said, 'That's a good picture, love. A bloody good picture!' and she had run away, frightened by his swear word.

She sprayed air freshener around. She opened other doors and expected the worst but a skin of dust lay over every room except the one in which Cliff slept. Inside another, boxes were stacked. She brushed away the dust from one and opened it. Inside were whole bottles and broken pieces of blue, green and amber glass slicing against each other. Gran's bottle collection. She lifted out two bottles, unbroken, blue and green, and held them to the light and turned them. She took them to her old bedroom at the front of the house and set them on the sill of the window where they consumed the morning light and sent it skipping, changed, across the floor. The blue bottle had a story associated with it but she couldn't remember what it was.

She went back to the room and opened another box and peered inside. It was piled high with loose photographs. She looked through them. There were old photographs which she had never seen before: her parents, her and Cliff as children. Someone had emptied every album in the house into the box. She opened an envelope lying loose among the photos. Her wedding photos; the ones she had sent Cliff in the mail. There was one of her and Thomas with Cliff before the reception; before Cliff had started to drink. She closed her eyes at the memory, smiled and shook her head. It was years ago now. Cliff had met Thomas for the first time on the wedding day and they had taken an instant dislike to each other. It had been hard to convince Cliff to come at all and he nearly went home then. Later, they both wished he had. She had persuaded him to stay. He had started drinking as soon as he arrived at the reception. After the speeches he had picked a fight with one of Thomas's friends and fallen and hit himself against the corner of one of the tables. He had come to apologise, she thought, stumbling his way across the room, blood snaking out of his nose, spattering across the table, across the cake.

Unintentional. Maybe.

She had never wanted a wedding. It was Thomas's idea. He wanted his friends to have a good time; music and dancing, but family had spoiled that. Later, Thomas's smirk when he remembered it always made her angry. She had forgiven Cliff as far as she was able, and told him so, but he had been silent about it. She had wondered if he even remembered it. He had gone home and there was no one there—here—to remind him.

She left the room and closed the door. She looked into the bathroom. The big metal bathtub still sat against the wall. Two columns of blue glass shinnied up beside the centre panes of the window just as they always had. She was surprised to see thriving plants, their tender tips searching around the walls, out through cracks between the window and the wall.

She imagined the tub brimming with steaming water. She checked the door. It had a lock, *and* a key. She walked softly back through the house anticipating hot water up to her chin. She felt better about staying. She and Cliff would sort things out.

She collected her suitcase from the car. She lifted her head and looked at the view but her heart didn't sink as she had expected it to. There was nothing there to be afraid of.

She put the suitcase down in the room. The bed was stripped and bare but for a pillow. She opened one of the windows, closed the door, and lay down on the bed. Paint had started to peel from the ceiling. She could see old and secret graffiti scratched into the bedhead but couldn't remember what it meant. She listened but heard nothing but a dog barking somewhere. She waited for Cliff to come home.

A breeze blew outside and puffed against the curtains, swirled through the room. It caressed her face and deepened her breathing.

She fell asleep and dreamed. Her leg jumped. Sweat flowed and ran in wet lines down her neck and onto the bed.

Outside, the ocean was spotted with the breaking tips of swell like snow, sparkling in the sun, disappearing into nothing. Clouds drifted across the sky and split sunlight into shafts that whirled across the valley so quickly they might have been intentional, as if someone could look down and see things they recognised in the shifting light and shade.

Cliff and Daniel stayed at the waterhole for hours; smoking, talking. Daniel hung his head over the water and looked at his reflected face drained of colour, shaky. When he was thirsty Cliff drank from the creek and Daniel, after a while, did too. He was surprised they had so much to talk about. Cliff talked and Daniel listened. Everything came out. It seemed like years' worth of conversation. At school it had been different, Daniel talked, Cliff had listened, quietly, patiently. When the words dried up Cliff lay back in the sun. The wrinkles in his forehead seemed less, his muscles looser.

Daniel said, 'Can I stay for a while?'

Cliff looked at him strangely.

'Don't be stupid.'

'Thanks.'

'What about your job?'

'I'm working for my father.'

'Oh.'

'Why haven't you ever been back before?' Cliff said after a long pause.

'I don't know,' said Daniel. And that was the truth.

'Why did you go and work for your dad? I thought you didn't get along with him.'

'I don't, but things weren't working out. I was working in a cafe. I didn't like it. My girlfriend left me.'

'Ahhhh,' said Cliff, 'what happened?'

'I walked in on her, well, them.'

'What, doing it?'

'Yeah, I came home one day. The house was really quiet and I heard them. I was angry because I thought there was someone else in our room. I sneaked up. The door was open. She was on top of this guy.'

'Really?'

'Yeah. She said later it didn't mean anything. It was a sex thing. They had gone to school together.'

'Shit.'

'Yeah. But what got me was how happy she was, the look on her face, you know? She looked so *happy*, so beautiful and happy. I'd never seen her like that before.'

'That's too bad.'

'Yeah.'

'Did you love her?'

Daniel wondered why the question sounded so strange and then realised that he had never been able to answer it.

'I don't know,' he said.

They smoked some more.

Daniel said, 'Why didn't you ever leave?'

'Never got around to it. The country's just the same as the city anyway; there's just more space between people.'

Daniel smiled.

'And you don't change from place to place do you?'

'I suppose not.'

The air was clearer between them.

They walked back to the house; emerging from a different track that delivered them into the open paddock west of the house. They walked and Daniel kept his eyes open for cowshit and remembered Cliff's fondness for the surprise attack but none came. As they neared the house Daniel saw that its rear third was almost submerged under overgrown hedges and vines. A water tank stood red with rust. Cows grazed outside the barbed-wire fence that circled the house and the old farm sheds.

Lizards lay flat against boards, black eyed, baking in the afternoon sun, scattering when Cliff and Daniel's shadow passed across them, tasting the air with tiny tongues.

Cliff saw the car first. He didn't recognise it. Daniel watched his shoulders tense and the angle of his head change as he listened. They walked through the back door into the kitchen and then along the hallway. No one. No sound.

'Were you expecting someone?' Daniel whispered.

'No. I suppose it could be . . .'

'Who?'

'My sister.'

Susan. Daniel felt sick. He wished he could vanish.

There were two bedrooms at the front of the house; one on either side of the doorway. Both bedroom doors were closed. Cliff pointed to one door. He clicked the other open and peered inside and then pulled his head out. The door he had assigned to Daniel was locked. His sweating hand slid against the brass.

'It's locked,' he whispered.

Cliff grinned. 'Let's go round the front.'

They walked out onto the verandah and peered through the windows. She was asleep on the bed. Daniel remembered her face before he saw it.

Cliff rapped hard on the glass and she snapped upright, her head searching for the source of the noise. She saw Cliff's grinning grimy face and her eyes widened. They were white and huge. She swore at Cliff and threw the pillow at him. It made a soft puffing noise against the wall. She opened the door.

Daniel felt stupid.

'Didn't think I'd see you back here again,' said Cliff.

They pecked each other on the cheek and hugged awkwardly.

'Thought I'd better come and check up on you,' she said.

'Hello,' said Daniel, 'I'm Daniel, you probably don't remember me. I went to school with Cliff.'

'Hello.'

They stood awkwardly for a moment. Susan was still sleepy.

'On holidays?' Daniel asked.

'Yes, just for a couple of weeks or so. What about you?'

'I'm working at the moment but I was going to stay with Cliff for a few days. Unless it's not convenient.'

'Don't be silly. Don't let me change your plans. What work do you do?'

Daniel cringed. 'I'm selling aluminium siding for my father. What do you do?'

'I'm a photographer.'

'Really.'

'Yes, I have a business with my husband.'

Cliff stood with his arms folded and watched them chat. He seemed to be smiling at something as he scratched Curly's head.

'We were going to go get something to eat,' said Daniel. Do you want us to get you something or do you want to come too?'

'I'll come with you.'

She disappeared into the room. Daniel looked at Cliff, who shrugged back at him.

When she came out she looked neater. She had put on shoes and lipstick.

They drove into town in her car. Daniel sat in the back. He could see Cliff was uncomfortable with the clean seats and new smell. At the milk bar Cliff bought half a chicken, a hamburger and chips. Daniel bought a hamburger. Susan, finally, bought mineral water and a salad sandwich. They sat at a table in the park and ate together.

Daniel relaxed slightly.

Susan pointed to things that had changed and Cliff nodded and seemed surprised by some of the things she pointed out. Daniel could not tell whether he was happy to see her or not. He seemed content to listen. Daniel chatted to Susan. She was Cliff's older sister who he had loved in secret. He had written her letters and dreamt of her. He remembered the dreams and the letters. Their intensity had worried him. She had left Greenhill on a train and his mind like an addiction.

He remembered that. He was much older now. She seemed like an old friend. He thought it was a good thing to be.

They drove home. They were all tired. They sat in the kitchen and drank tea and coffee.

Daniel kept his eyes open until his hands began to jump. Soon, the conversation exhausted itself. Daniel was intrigued by the things Cliff and Susan *didn't* talk about. His thoughts wandered until he noticed the others were getting ready for sleep. He did the same.

Daniel lay on the mattress in the spare room wide awake with his ears laid open and listening for sounds in the house. He thought he would go out like a light but his eyes wouldn't shut and his mind would not stop thinking. Dread slid around his stomach. He tried to make a decision about tomorrow; whether he would stay or go. He heard Cliff's voice rumbling softly through the walls, but if there was an opposite pole to the conversation he could not hear it. Before the sound ended he had stopped listening and the house slept in the moonlit quiet.

I built a shack up there behind the house when I was a boy; butted against the tallest tree I could find. I would sleep up there, the creek, the sound of water all night around me, and I could see the world, all right, up the top of the tree, if I felt like climbing it. I could see the lights of the town through the leaves, could see the headland, where the river dropped out into the ocean, the brown mixing in with the blue. Sat up there and watched the cane fires, sniffing the smoke, watching just a glow in the sky miles away or hear the crack and hiss of one close by. I knew that snakes—brown and black— would be rippling out of the cane away from the flames. That was all you could see from the top of the tree and that was enough for me.

My father saw more, of course, he always did. Bunyips creeping along crevices, sniffing out seams of gold which they eat for ballast, heavier than rock to keep them weighed down in the dark water. He said those who had seen one surface from a summer pool remember the gold, stuck fast and gleaming between their teeth.

Daniel woke tingling with anticipation and with a sore back from the broken springs in the mattress. He met Susan in the hall. He was surprised how different she looked without makeup: sick, her eyes watery and pale.

'Good morning.'

'Good morning.'

She didn't look like she had slept very well.

He looked in the refrigerator out of habit. There wasn't much in there. He found cornflakes and ate them with milk.

Cliff and Susan came in and they made a loose circle around the kitchen table.

'We need to go shopping,' said Susan.

'Yeah. Okay.'

They waited for her to get ready. Cliff was bemused.

'What's she doing in there?'

'I don't know. What women do to get ready.'

They sat in the kitchen and smoked and looked at each other without speaking as friends sometimes do.

Susan took her time. She went to the toilet. Something caught her eye as she stood. Something moving, something big. A frog. A fat green frog. In the bowl where she'd just been sitting.

'God!' she said. She didn't like surprises. She walked into the kitchen and announced that there was a frog in the toilet. Cliff laughed at her and she belted his shoulder with her clenched fist but it only made him laugh harder.

She gave up.

Daniel thought she looked much healthier.

Cliff insisted on driving his car. Susan sat gingerly in the front seat. They drove into the town and parked in the street outside the supermarket.

'Why don't you park in the car park?' asked Susan.

'There's a bit of shade here.'

'But it's further to carry the bags.'

'There's three of us!'

'All right then, suit yourself.'

'I'll wait out here for you.'

'You're a big help!' said Susan. 'Daniel, can you come and help?'

'Sure.'

Cliff leaned against the car and looked up and down the street and gauged the distance to the nearest hotel and the time it would take him to get there and back and what he could do in the meantime. Perfectly preserved old ladies walking along the footpath approached him cautiously but he didn't notice. Small children stared at him and he stared back and made faces. His leather jacket was a hot skin across his back.

He needed a drink. He needed to sit down. He compromised and walked to the bottle shop and bought a carton of cold beer. He leaned against the car, opened the carton, extracted a bottle and drank it.

Inside, in the cool air of the supermarket, Daniel pushed the trolley and Susan selected from the shelves and tut tutted to herself when she couldn't find something on the list. Daniel smiled to himself as he tried not to look at her too closely. Her concentration fascinated him. Shopping. He could feel eyes watching but Susan seemed oblivious. He wondered what it would be like to be married.

He tried to see the resemblance between her and Cliff. He peered at her sideways and she startled him with a question.

'How long have you known Cliff?'

'We went through school together.'

'I think I remember you. My grandparents never let Cliff's friends inside but I suppose you knew that. But, looking at you now, I think I do recognise you.'

'Long hair. Dirty.'

'You were all dirty,' she laughed, 'and cheeky. I wanted to kill some of you!'

She picked up two packets of pasta.

'Sorry,' Daniel said, 'I do remember you shouting a lot.'

'Nothing to be sorry about.'

'Well, there were things actually. We were always trying to see you naked.'

He held his breath.

'Oh, I know you were. But you never did, did you?'

'No.'

A packet of self-raising flour.

'Did you see what he's done to the walls in the living room?'

'Yep.'

'What do you think?'

'I don't know. I didn't know he could paint but, you know,

53

I haven't seen him in nearly ten years, I don't know a lot of things about him.'

'Neither do I,' said Susan.

They finished the shopping and loaded the bags into the car. Cliff eyed them both from under his untidy fringe.

'Come on,' said Susan, sidling off up the street.

'Did you get ice-cream?' asked Cliff.

'Yes.'

'It'll melt in the car!'

'Not if we're quick. Come on!'

They walked along the street until they came to a butchery. It was an old brick building and inside there was sawdust on the floor, and out the back Daniel could see stainless steel machines; blood, and knives. Green tiles lined the walls and framed the window through which Cliff stared, smoking. The butcher came out and his eyes narrowed into fierce slits when he saw Cliff.

'No smoking in here mate!'

Cliff peered at him and threw the cigarette on the floor where it lay, still burning. He flung the door open and stalked out. Susan's face was tight and Daniel saw her shake her head almost imperceptibly. He followed Cliff out.

'What's your problem?'

'Guy's a fuck.'

They drove home in silence. Susan noticed a market in full swing in the park by the river. As soon as they had emptied the car of the shopping she climbed into her own car and drove back down to the market.

It was busy. People were stopping by as they drove down to the beach or on their way back from there. Some were buying fish and chips at the shop and sitting on the grass to eat and watch people go by.

There were stalls of old books, bric-a-brac, craft, plants, clothes. Food sat on tables surrounded by bronzed women with grubby children. Older women sat fanning themselves and selling cakes wrapped tightly in plastic and sweating slightly under the cloudy sky. She recognised a few people but most were strangers. She walked through the loose rows of tables and ducked into hedges of clothes. A barbecue sizzled somewhere and thick, smell-laden smoke blew over people's heads and across the river.

She couldn't believe how much Greenhill had changed since she had last been here. There were all kinds of people now. Undesirables. Men leaned out of the windows of the hotel diagonal to the park and watched proceedings like a jury.

She felt eyes on her and felt uncomfortably conspicuous. Youths with blank looks sidled around and past her. She could smell them, some with their heads down, some brazen and daring her to look them in the eye. She ducked into a stall and breathed the warm smell of canvas. Stall owners eyed the steady lines walking between the rows. She felt slightly ridiculous hiding from a few grubby children.

She remembered seeing the circus here as a child, and being frightened by toothy monkeys and sweating clowns. The trapeze artists had been the only act that had stopped her running from the tent. She remembered how much she had wanted to be one, spinning at the end of a rope in red feathers and sequins.

A tall man with dark smeary tattoos minded a stall of frothy pink and blue baby clothes. A second-hand bookseller spruiked half forgotten stories; adventures and romances heaped in a pile on his rickety table. His voice lost in the murmur of the crowd. Girls with bare, brown midriffs wound through the crowd like eastern dancers, oblivious to stares, some with babies on their hips. Two stout women sat at a table and stared at the young women as they walked past, leaning towards each other and smirking behind hands which otherwise picked at faces or waved away flies.

The youths rolled around again, tattooed and pierced, cigarettes sprouting from their mouths. They seemed to carry everything they needed around with them in deep pockets and even though it was hot they wore long pants and had jackets tied around their waists as if ready to move to a cooler place at short notice. They walked through the stalls without stopping, as if they were going somewhere, unsmiling, then stopped when they reached open spaces. They seemed to be waiting for suggestions from each other as to how to spend the rest of the day.

Susan walked in the opposite direction and saw a group of young girls eating ice-cream from pink cones. She looked around and spied the ice-cream van and went over and brought herself a double coner; licking the sticky peak and smiling to herself. She felt anxious about going back to the house. She was glad Daniel was there: she hoped he would be an incentive for her and Cliff not to fight.

She sat on the grass and watched one of the girls cross a stretch of grass in a series of graceful little leaps. Her feet were bare and her legs and arms were buttered brown. She was of that age that adults find so hard to remember; her dress would be too small for her in a year or two. Fresh flowers radiated from her fist. She made it to the edge of the grass, past the prickles, with her eyes down, flicking the hair from her face with her free hand and balancing on one leg between each jump. She stopped and looked up and saw Susan sitting in the shade watching and her face creased in a smile; an open, toothy smile that there seemed to be little reason for until Susan realised it was a reflection of the one plastered across her own. She waved to the girl, who waved back and ran down the street after her friends. Too late, she remembered her camera, snug in her bag.

Susan wondered if she had ever seen anyone as free of care as the girl. She stood and walked away and did not look back.

A crowd was forming in the park. She couldn't see what they were watching until she moved closer and saw the busker going through his routine on the grass. She watched him juggle, joke, walk on his hands and backflip. He made the kids laugh. When she finished she slipped through the crush of children and dropped money into his hat and kept walking.

Clouds slipped across the sky like a blanket. People drifted away. Susan looked around then walked over to the road. She strode up the footpath until she reached his street. Her fingers tingled as she followed the old map in her head, familiar to her feet, to the end of the street.

His house was there but not there. It was a worn and sagging shell; lifeless and grey. Boards covered windows. The roof had collapsed over the door and leaves were piled in the gutters. She could see black scorch marks at the tops of the windows. It looked like it had been that way for years. She was barely surprised.

'Did you burn your own house down you stupid careless bastard?' she asked.

It seemed likely; even though she did not even know if he had been living there at the time of the fire, it felt like an appropriate conclusion.

'You were always careless,' she said, and took out her camera and carefully focused and pressed the release.

She saw a woman watching her from the yard next door. She was half-hidden by bushes and when Susan saw her she pretended to be preoccupied with something Susan couldn't see.

'Did you know them, lovey?' she said as curiosity got the better of her.

'Yes,' answered Susan, 'well, I knew them about ten years ago.'

'Little kiddie died in there a few years back. Her father burnt his hands trying to get her out.'

Susan held her breath. 'Do you remember their name?'

'His name was Michael something. Can't remember the little girl's name, or the mother's now, come to think of it.'

'Do you know where they went? What happened to them?'

'No, sorry lovey, I don't. Sorry.'

'Well, thanks,' Susan said, and walked back the way she had come.

She knew nothing of his life here. Nothing about a child. She tried to imagine him in the house with them. She could see him sitting around a table but the other faces could only be guesses. She felt sad but her sadness was diluted by the years that had passed.

She walked through the park as the light failed and people started to pack up their stalls. Thunder echoed down the valley. She reached the bridge and as she crossed it she reckoned the amount of time she had before the storm broke. Not much, she thought, and she remembered a girl running against the clock under a sky filled to the brim with enchantment.

The railway line lay like a ruler across the flat land past the bridge. Next to the track was the road and the red-brick railway station. There were a few lonely houses. She could hear kids yelling and fighting and adult voices raised and then quiet again. An old man sat in the darkness of his verandah watching her walk past. She saw the tip of his cigarette flare and fade.

The storm began to flicker and close in on the town. Lightning tapped the earth like a kid with a stick on a beach. The street changed from bumpy bitumen to dust. She remembered seeing children playing in the dirt at the edge of the street and buying ice blocks from the shop that wasn't there any more; standing and watching the ants find the sweet red drips as the ice melted.

She passed the pumping station and heard its comforting, civilised hum. She saw the showground ahead and quickened her stride until she reached the fence which surrounded it. The fence was falling apart and she found a loose section and slipped through. She walked past the larger pavilions towards a muddled group of smaller tin sheds. She heard voices and it was a second before her legs stopped, frozen. There's no reason for anyone to be here, she thought. There was only the barest skeleton of a reason for her to be there. She stood and listened but before she heard the voices again she saw their owners, huddled under the eaves of a shed. She twisted on the grass but saw them rise in unison and walk towards her silently.

She noticed paint on the buildings was peeling and rust was eating into the edges of things. The cooler backs of some of the buildings were covered in the same vines that blanketed the river banks. She could see houses, minutes away.

They surrounded her in seconds, the same boys from the park. She kept walking.

'Hi, honey.'

'Hi, baby.'

'Where are you going?'

'What's the matter?'

'Why won't you talk to us?'

They were enjoying her fear and that made her face burn. They began to pluck at the bag hanging off her shoulder, at her arm, touching her arse and legs.

She wanted to swear at them but her jaw felt frozen, the muscles in her neck slippery. She got her mouth open but no sound came out.

'Give head, baby?'

A thought struck her. Once, she had followed Michael into every one of the buildings, despite their locks and bars. It was the reason why they had needed to break in that had lured her back once more; to see what lingered and what had gone.

What she remembered held complete panic at bay. She changed direction. Rain began to fall and thunder crashed overhead. The boys enjoyed the game, they yelped and whooped and pushed each other around. She remembered she and Michael used to slide under one building. Maybe that one. She could see a dark gap near the ground and the sharp-looking edges of the tin. The boys seemed as curious as they were cowardly. She veered closer to the building and dived at the gap. She knew her aim was out and felt the tin slice through her clothes and shockingly, sickeningly, into her back. She felt their hands around her ankles and she kicked and the anger that wouldn't come out of her mouth came kicking and thrashing out through her feet. They let go. She scrambled along the bare earth in absolute blackness. How far? Which direction? Her memory failed her. She struggled forward and pushed up against the boards over her head with one hand. Adrenalin kept her going. What she was doing seemed ridiculous beyond words. She wanted to giggle madly. Someone call a cab, I'm going home to my nice warm bed, she thought.

She pushed against a board and it moved, slightly. She stopped and flipped onto her back and pushed up with both her arms. The board moved up. She pushed and bent at the waist and found herself sitting with her head in clear space, the outlines of windows high on the walls. She stood and stepped out and the board slammed back into place. She sat down on it. She could hear them shouting at each other. Sliding through the dirt. She heard them bumping against the boards, rattling the door and throwing their bodies against it.

The storm broke overhead. Rain streamed against the windows. She prayed they were high enough not to be climbed through. She couldn't hear them any more. Minutes went by and dragged into an hour. She began to shiver. Her teeth clicked together. Pain in her back began to cramp the muscles there. She heard a sound through the rain, maybe of tearing metal. It stopped and then the rain stopped as quickly as it had started. They were still outside. She could hear them arguing. After a silence a voice spoke clearly and close.

'Just give us your money and we'll go, okay?'

He was directly in front of her. The door.

'Push your money under the door.'

She felt glued to the board. If there was a boy under there he was being very quiet. A good little boy.

'Okay. But. Please. Go.'

The sentence separated. She had no control over each word. She didn't recognise her voice.

'Yeah, no worries lady. We won't hurt you.'

You have already, she thought.

She leaned forward and stood. Her legs were stiff and shaky and she took a step forward and listened for the sound of the board moving behind her but heard nothing. She took one step at a time, as softly as she could, but the boards still creaked under her weight. She reached into her bag for her purse and plucked notes from it. She had no idea how much money there was. A hundred maybe, two hundred? Enough to go anywhere in the country, get drunk for a week, whatever they wanted.

In the gloom she saw a flash of white in the keyhole of the door. An eye, watching her. She rushed forward and thrust the money through the hole they had made in the tin. A hand grabbed it and she heard running feet. She ran to the loose board and sat back down on it.

Feeling crept through her body. She waited, a different kind of anxiety took hold of her. She followed the tiny glowing points on the hands of her watch. Hours passed.

So much time.

She hummed a faintly happy tune.

She and Michael had spent hours in here when they should

have been at school. Hours and hours. Talking mostly, but about what she couldn't remember. Teasing each other with words. Trying to say what they meant without using the words which would have conveyed their meaning in a flash.

She remembered when they had come here after painters had been and even as his fingers had disappeared inside her she had fainted, sick from the fumes.

She could see him sitting in front of her. His uncomplicated smile a drug she had happily surrendered to.

Calm enveloped her. She wondered if she were in shock. She reached into the bag for the camera, took it out, held it out in front of her body, closed her eyes and released the shutter. She saw the light flash red through her eyelids.

She moved off the board and lifted it and dropped down onto the earth. The air was cool and fresh. She wriggled out on her stomach, dragging her bag behind her. The outside world glowed in front of her and she stopped as she reached it and looked out. The moon was up. There was no one in sight. She stood and walked as quickly as she could towards the houses and the river. She wanted to be able to swim for it if she had to. Tears ran down her cheeks and she sobbed as she walked. Her back burned. She reached the river and then turned towards the bridge and hugged the bank of the river. She saw no one and heard nothing alarming.

She crossed the bridge and followed streetlights to where her car was parked. Cars passed on the street but she kept her head straight and walked quickly. She unlocked the car and drove back to the house.

It was empty.

There was a note in Cliff's distinctive handwriting on the kitchen table.

Sorry, couldn't wait, it said. *Gone to the pub.*

She went into the bathroom, locked the door and pulled her top carefully over her shoulders. She could see a scrape between her shoulder blade nearly as large as her hand. Tiny red poppies of blood had formed and dried on the skin. She tried to clean the wound with soap but the angle was too sharp. She sat and thought, despairingly, of Thomas's gentle, precise touch.

Daniel and Cliff crossed the street from one hotel to another. Cliff tripped into the street and stepped in front of a car and the driver blared his horn, hung his head out the window and swore. It was hot despite the quick storm. Daniel stumbled along in Cliff's wake, looking carefully each way for cars, aware of the hardness around him and how fragile his body was. He still didn't feel right about not waiting for Susan. He wondered where she was.

'She can look after herself,' Cliff had said.

Daniel didn't feel too drunk. Cliff had overtaken him early on, impatient with his slow sips.

Music floated out through the hotel doors. They stepped inside. Well-dressed girls sat perched on stools while their boyfriends leant and bullshitted to each other at the bar. A thick-limbed doorman watched them as they walked in then turned away. Daniel felt underdressed in his jeans and T-shirt. Cliff wore his leather jacket, dirty jeans and greasy work boots. Daniel smelt sweat and beer and smoke. The band was loud and the windows that looked out on to the street were clouded over with condensation.

Cliff saw Jade weaving through the mob around the band with a beer glass in her hand. Men watched her; turned to their mates and muttered and some leered and laughed. Cliff slowed his drinking down a notch and went and leant against a carpeted wall.

Daniel skirted tables and headed for the bar. He overheard sentences in conversations. Plans, deals, judgments. He saw people looking at him and they didn't turn away as he met their eyes. He bought two more beers and turned to find Cliff. He was surprised to find him standing quietly, a thoughtful look on his face. He was watching something.

The band took a break. Daniel watched the crowd feed through the doors and out into the fresh air of the beer garden. He saw a girl standing by herself near the wall. She turned around and smiled at something with a slightly crooked smile that suggested more than amusement. She wore a mass of bangles and necklaces and earrings. It was her Cliff was watching.

'Do you know her?' Daniel shouted.

'No.'

'But you'd like to?'

Cliff said nothing.

'Go and say hello or something.'

'Go and get us another drink.'

'I just did.'

They stood and drank. Cliff still said nothing. Daniel began to feel bored and irritated. He went to the bar and bought more drinks.

'Do you know her name?' he asked the bartender and pointed.

'Jade,' the guy said, without hesitation, and gave him his change.

The band were back. They sounded better than before.

Cliff was swaying slightly and Daniel didn't know whether it was the music or the alcohol. He was starting to feel dizzy himself. He wanted to sit down but there were no free seats.

'Her name's Jade,' Daniel yelled, and that got Cliff's attention.

'How do you know?'

'I asked her.'

'No you didn't.'

'I'm psychic then. Go and ask her to dance. Go on!'

She was surrounded by men. One of them looked as though he was buying her drinks. Her hand moved steadily from the table to her mouth like a lift. There was a burly guy next to her, his body leaning over her and the table. He looked much older than the others. He was shouting into her ear but she seemed to be ignoring him. He had a thick beard and oily-looking hair. His arms stuck beefily from his rolled-up sleeves. There was a thick silver diver's watch on his wrist and he had a bad haircut. Daniel tried to watch them as casually as he could.

Cliff sat down on the floor. The crowd stepped over him. He bent one long leg; drew it up to touch his chin and then locked his arm around it. His other arm hung slack; pale and smoking at the tip. The band played on. The burly man and Jade danced. Daniel stepped onto the floor and started to dance near them. He could see that Jade was drunker than he was. She fell against the men. They didn't mind catching her. He moved across the floor until he was directly behind Jade and the man. The band began a faster song and the dancers danced faster. The burly man threw Jade into the air, and kissed her on the mouth when she came down. Daniel could see his fat pink tongue plunging into her mouth and strings of saliva falling into his beard as they parted. Daniel tried to spot Cliff. He saw him staring at them through his thick glasses, blowing smoke through his nostrils like a sleepy dragon.

Daniel turned back to the stage and was struck sideways by flying arms, cool, unguided, and slick with perspiration. Stunned, he turned and Jade was beside him, leaning against him. He could feel her heat, saw her half-closed eyes, her smell like an envelope around him. Her arm reached out and grabbed the back of his head and pulled it toward hers and kissed him. He felt her tongue against his teeth then she was gone, his lips damp from her. Something hard and heavy careered into the side of his head. He saw flashes of white dissolving into black.

He woke on the footpath outside. His face felt hot and wet. A breeze blew on his skin and cooled it. That breeze—that air—always made him think of Sylvia, and as he did he became even more disoriented.

Cliff's blurred outline pulled him up and propelled him stumbling along the road. Daniel thought he could see Jade running along with them. She grabbed his arm and helped carry him. He could hear metal against metal.

They ran out into the darkness along the road. They had walked down from the house so Cliff wouldn't be tempted to drive home at the end of the night. They walked and walked until Daniel was sure that the house had to be close. They stopped and sat down and his head began to clear.

'Shit, what happened?' he croaked.

'Someone hit you,' said a female voice.

'Yeah, I know that.'

'Don't worry, mate. I got him good for you,' said Cliff.

'I can't hear properly.'

'No, the gutless prick king hit you.'

'Who was the prick?'

'Just some prick.'

Daniel could hear something like running water, something like a song.

When he could stand they continued along the road. Soon, Daniel walked unaided. The night was beautifully clear after the storm. Stars surged overhead.

Cliff and Jade walked ahead of him. She seemed to have dropped into their orbit out of the sky. He saw them stop and walk to the side of the road, then Cliff leapt over the fence, his black boots on the wire. Jade leant against a fence post. Daniel caught up. He sat down in the wet grass and felt his head with his hands. Cliff moved out across the paddock toward a clump of trees. Black shapes moved among the blacker shadows. Cliff wheeled around them casually. They started to move off, disturbed. Heavy bodies rustled through the undergrowth.

Cows.

Daniel shook his head.

Suddenly Cliff ran directly at the herd. He had his shirt off and had picked up a long stick and was waving it around his head. Jade laughed, her body twisting against the fence post.

The herd bolted. Cliff ran after them, surprising Daniel with his easy speed. Cliff caught one by the tail and it bellowed. He threw away the stick and took two long running steps and threw himself across the animal's back. The cow ran with the strange and pale cargo of Cliff clinging to its back like a limpet.

Jade laughed hysterically.

Daniel laughed as well, even though he had seen this trick before, and even though his head felt like someone had dropped something on it from a great height.

One night the ferry broke down and we all decided to swim across the river. It was a challenge for my father and he loved that. We were all strong swimmers, my father, my sister and I. The moon was full. I can still see them, slipping through the black water, silent to save their breath, nothing above them and nothing below. My sister stopped in the middle, tired. I held her from behind, my arm across her chest, holding her head back and telling her to rest. She recovered her strength and we continued. Father was nearly across. She smiled at me. Somewhere between the middle and the bank she disappeared, without a sound. We searched, dived deep into the water for her but she was lost. I remember it clearly.

I often wonder how it was to be her, swimming across the river with her father and brother, still young and strong, drowning, but I have never had much of an idea because, back then, I barely knew her.

Father never spoke of it to anyone. Not my mother. He changed then, there on the river. It was a wedge, something that kept his mind open so things came and went that shouldn't have.

He became an inventor later. Machines, their purposes hidden to everyone but himself. He could see it. He would build fabulous steam-powered contraptions that never worked. Then electricity came along and everything changed. He couldn't get his mind around it. 'How can you get your mind around lightning?' he would say. He would spend all day roaming the countryside looking for material or putting things together in the shed. His was an entertaining madness, feeding on itself. He was as normal as the next person when he came inside the house and then he would discuss his plans and theories and cover the kitchen table with pencil lead sketches.

When an invention failed he would bury it. 'A decent burial,' he would say. We don't know how he did it. We don't know where they are buried. All over the place.

He took to riding trains, jumping on them where they slowed near the farm, up and down the coast. Writing down what people said to him. He said they were clues. Messages as to where to go. One night he ran from the house at speed and disappeared into the night. Several people said they heard him coming, saw him leaping over the old stone fences, across their farms. When they finally found him a day later he was ten miles away and dead. He was eighty-six.

How's that.

There was one invention that worked, or seemed to. When he died I threw it into the pool where no one would ever find it. As far as I know that was the only one that worked. No one ever guessed what it did.

Susan heard them coming. It was past midnight. She lay on her bed with a sharp knife from the kitchen in her hand. She heard laughing. A girl laughing. She felt relieved and annoyed at once. They sounded drunk. They crashed up the stairs and down the hall. She went to the door, opened it, and stepped out. Cliff saw her and reeled off an explanation.

'Daniel got belted. We're goin' down to the beach.'

Susan looked at Daniel in the dim light. His cheek was red and puffy but his eyes seemed clear and he looked at her steadily.

'What happened?'

'Some prick king hit him.'

'Russell,' said Jade. Cliff looked at her.

'Why?'

'He's stupid. Cliff belted Russell back.'

Susan looked at Daniel under the kitchen light. It didn't look too serious. Her back throbbed as she moved. She could smell the unmistakable smell of cattle.

'What have you been doing?'

'We had a rodeo,' Cliff said and giggled and Jade giggled with him.

'Sorry, I didn't catch your name.'

'Jade.'

'Hello Jade, I'm Susan. What did you say about the beach, Cliff?'

'We're going for a swim.'

'Now?'

'Yep.'

Cliff snaked out his arm across her shoulders. Pain grabbed her. She felt faint.

'What's the matter Sus?'

'Nothing. A box fell on me, it's okay.'

'Show me!'

'No, Cliff!'

He pulled at her top and peered down her back. He swayed into the bathroom and came back with a bottle of iodine. He unscrewed the cap and the bottle spilled from his fingers and half the contents ran out onto the kitchen table before Daniel could right it.

'Let me,' Daniel said. 'What about your shirt? This stuff stains.'

'Don't worry about it.'

Daniel found a cotton ball in the bathroom and held it to the mouth of the bottle. He dabbed it on to her broken skin as gently as he could and soon the area was dark orange. Cliff and Jade watched, fascinated. Daniel felt like a surgeon. When he had finished she said thank you.

'Okay, we'll go now,' said Cliff.

'You can't drive to the beach, Cliff! None of you can.'

'You come then. Because we're going anyway.'

Susan knew better than to argue with Cliff. She looked at Daniel.

'Do you want to go to the beach?'

'Yes,' he said, 'I'm not tired.'

'Okay then, everyone get in my car.'

Cliff grinned at her.

She didn't want to stay in the house by herself any longer. The beach was preferable.

Cliff and Jade yelped like kids and galloped down the hall and into the car.

Daniel followed more slowly. Susan picked up her bag, locked the bedroom door and turned out the light.

They drove along the track, Cliff directing Susan although she knew the way perfectly. The trees and bushes on either side of the road were covered in fine white dust. Moths fluttered in the headlights. Daniel sat quietly in the front seat and watched things go by. They saw the glowing eyes of a pack of dogs loping their way through the low scrub. Daniel thought he saw Curly but Cliff was unconvinced.

They stopped and piled out. The beach was deserted and as wide as a highway.

'Last one in's a roaring mongrel!' yelled Cliff.

He took off his shirt, dropped his pants, and pounded

towards the surf, his white arse flashing. Jade did the same. Daniel tried to look somewhere else. He saw a large brown mole on the inside of her thigh.

'Be careful!' yelled Susan.

Daniel sat down. There was a thin crust of damp sand which broke as he touched it. Underneath it was still warm. He ran his fingers through it. He wanted to put his head down and sleep but he wanted to feel water as well. Susan walked along the water's edge with her shoes in her hand.

He stood and fumbled with the buttons on his shirt. He broke some and threw his shirt onto the sand and promptly overbalanced and toppled to the ground. He rolled onto his back and looked up. He wasn't going anywhere. He moved his head and saw something like glitter shifting around behind his eyes. He lay still and the sky began to float down to meet him halfway. The moon hung scarred and waterless in the black.

Seas of tranquillity.

He closed his eyes. When he opened them Susan was bending over him.

'Are you all right?'

'Yeah, I'm okay, I think.'

'Are you going in?'

'Maybe.'

'Want a hand?'

She took hold of his hand and helped him up. They walked down to the water and stepped over the first wave together. The water was cool on their feet and hissed across the sand. Daniel could see Jade and Cliff disappearing under the waves farther out. He stopped with the water at his knees and watched them. He could hear the jingle of Jade's jewellery as she jumped over waves. Cliff lifted her from the waist and threw her up into the air. When she stood beside him she came up to his shoulder. He wondered if Cliff had seen the kiss she had given him. She was a strange girl. He liked her already. He turned and watched the beach.

Susan gave in to temptation and sank to her knees in the surf and let the foaming water wash over her. The salt stung her back and made it burn. Fear floated away like a bad dream and what was left intoxicated her with a dizzying intensity. She glanced at Daniel over her shoulder and kept her distance. Once she had swum here with Michael, his body flashing as he dived around her, making fun of her paleness. They would lie close and she would brush her lips against the ocean water beaded on his skin. She remembered the taste of his mouth, the sound of his laugh, his bad lies. She had been fearless with him and she felt fearless now. She wanted to shout.

She floated on her back and sound faded and she was completely alone. The sky was not black but a lattice of the deepest blue that stars gleamed through. It promised nothing and everything.

Cliff and Jade stayed in the ocean. Daniel, and then Susan, left the water and sat some distance away from the pile of clothes on the beach. Neither spoke to the other. Susan smiled at Daniel and wrapped herself in a towel.

Eventually, Cliff emerged from the water and ran directly to his clothes. He put them on and then walked down to the high-tide line and dragged back a log of driftwood. He disappeared into the bush behind them and came back with an armful of reasonably dry wood and threw it against the log and lit the pile with his lighter. Finally, some sticks caught and he placed more wood over the flames until they were roaring and sending sparks spinning down the beach.

They could still see Jade in the water; spreadeagled in the shallows. She was facing away from the ocean where no one watched. Small waves reached and washed over her.

'Come on,' Cliff shouted to her.

Finally she stood and walked toward them, stopping to investigate things washed up at the tide line. She picked up her clothes and stood in the firelight. She threw objects onto the sand and put on her clothes.

'What's that?' she said, and pointed.

'A cuttlefish bone,' said Daniel. 'They have green blood and three hearts. They change colour to match their surroundings. Like a chameleon.'

Cliff stared at him and Daniel smiled back.

'Can they change sex?'

'No, I don't think so.'

Jade sat next to Cliff and ran her fingers speculatively across his bare back as if they were alone on the beach. Soon, Daniel saw her polish Cliff's gold fillings with her tongue.

'Come on, time to go!' Susan almost shouted.

She drove them back to the house. Curly watched them as they walked into the house, sniffed, then licked their salty limbs before curling up near the television.

'See, it wasn't Curly,' said Cliff, and disappeared into his room with Jade.

Susan slipped into the bathroom. Daniel heard the shower come on. She emerged with her hair wet. She said goodnight to Daniel and went to bed, leaving a clean smell in her wake. Daniel, after sitting alone at the table for a minute, went into his room, looked at the misshapen mattress on the floor and looked for a blanket, but couldn't find one. Finally, exasperated, he curled up under his jacket and tried to go to sleep.

Jade lay across Cliff's bed. She looked small, like a kid. She peered at him standing with his hands on his hips, watching her.

'What's so funny?'

'You,' she said.

He wanted to reach out and touch the bones at the top of her chest but she was still a stranger. He felt sober, awkward.

His reputation around town had nothing to do with women. Everything he wanted to say came out the wrong way before he had said it. She laughed again.

Cliff smiled, frozen. Something had to rush in, replace the uncertainty, before he ran from the room.

She reached out to him, each arm a cluster of silver. They held each other and the metal was a bridge between them, digging coolly into flesh. The ends of chains dangled from her wrists, neck and ankles like tiny pendulums.

'Why don't you take them off,' he said.

'I'd feel naked without them,' she said and laughed.

Questions had to wait.

Jade reached and switched off the lamp which stood on the table next to the bed.

Daniel heard them. Laughter and then silence and then words and then sounds looping and repeating, meaningless to a listener in the dark. The sounds stopped and he wondered, in the silence, if he had only imagined them.

He eased off the bed and tiptoed to the door and tried to open it without it creaking but failed. He rolled his feet up the hall and out onto the verandah. An armchair sat hunched in the corner. He wanted a cigarette but not badly enough to blunder around in the dark looking for one. His chest hurt anyway.

He could hear a humming noise, as if the house slumbered over engines running deep underground. He held his hands over his ears and the sound increased. He listened to it, recognised its rhythm, closed his eyes and, finally, fell asleep.

Michael dozed fitfully beside a creek. Possums screeching in the trees over his head kept him awake. His head felt like an oven and his chest rasped and burnt as he breathed. He coughed and dust from his blanket got up his nose and made him sneeze. The ground was as hard as steel and ground into his fleshless body. Mosquitoes whined around his head and hunger gnawed at his guts like a dog.

When he slept his dream arms stoked a furnace until they blackened and charred and gave off blue and orange flames and the flesh of his chest sealed and smoked like a prime cut and he woke with a name stillborn on the end of his tongue.

Just before dawn Jade sprung upright from the waist. Her head was thick and untidy. She eyed the dark shape of the man beside her. He was lying face down. Moles on his back like a map of the night sky. The darker shapes of his tattoos against the blades in his shoulders. She leaned across and breathed in his smell. A muscle in his back jumped, twitched and kept twitching like a dog dreaming of a chase.

She slipped off the bed and felt her way along its edge toward the door. She took the towel hanging on the doorknob, wrapped it around her, opened the door and navigated by running an open palm along the wall. Doorways glowed at either end of the house. She found the kitchen and drank from the tap over the sink. She walked out the door and down the back steps onto the grass. Ragged cloud doused the moon's light. Wind rushed in the trees. She was ready to run but breathed deeply and the feeling left her. Her bladder was full. She turned and faced the house, squatted, pissed. When she stood rain was falling, slapping flat against her bare shoulders. She ran into the house. The rain came down harder, bouncing off the opaque awning she stood under near the back step. She listened to the sound; then crossed her arms and went back into the room.

TWO

Charms and confusions

The days that followed were clear and bright. Warm air settled in the valley until the afternoon breeze off the ocean threaded its way across the land like a tide and pulled curtains through open windows until the sun set. Night sounds measured the darkness as no clock could. Children lay in their beds anticipating holidays under the sun and others dreamt of imaginary worlds which glistened in their heads like coloured stones.

In the house on the hill Cliff and Jade met at the end of each day and disappeared into their room before doing anything else.

Jade lit sticks of incense from the fading embers of others. Blue smoke drifted around, sank like gas through cracks in the floor and disappeared into the dry earth beneath. She loved the view from the verandah. She refused Cliff nothing and spent hours sleeping, recovering. She dreamt of a tiny man cradled in her arm; guileless and perfect. When they were awake together she let her mind wander and forgot his questions. He thought it was cute. They heard voices and sometimes, laughter, ripple through the door. Floorboards creaked a different tune as Daniel or Susan walked past.

Susan enjoyed the sun and found quiet corners of the house to avoid the others. She cooked her favourite meals whenever she felt like eating them. Thomas rang the house but she refused to discuss anything with him. 'I need more time,' she told him. She considered telling the police what had happened at the shed but decided against it. She considered telling the others, but that too seemed pointless. Instead, despite the sense of power she had felt on the beach, she jumped at every noise, locked her door and kept her windows shut. The quietness of the house during the day sent her to sleep where she sat. Shadows shifted around her. Familiar smells crept up on her between footsteps and disappeared between others. She visited her grandfather. The house seemed to belong to her again.

When the blackened skin of his cheekbone had faded to a cloudy purple, Daniel continued to criss-cross the district with his portfolio of before and after aluminium siding pictures tucked under his arm. He was half-hearted and anxious and couldn't explain why. He couldn't bring himself to approach anyone who lived in a house made of wood. Even if the house was falling apart, he thought it had more character than a hundred brick houses. He spent more and more of each day lying under a tree that grew on a hill overlooking the valley and the sea.

In Greenhill he bought bread fresh from the oven, smiling and breathless in front of the bakery's glass counter.

People looked at his hair and his face and then sideways and through him. He began to do the same to them.

Someone in the house wrote on blue-lined paper looking out an open window:

My perfect lover:
Would know exactly where to touch me and when.
Would dress up and put on a show for me if I asked,
(nicely).

Could keep a secret.
Be as loyal as I am, (sometimes).
Would know what desire meant.
Would not be afraid of anything I was.
Would have good rhythm.
Would know to see past the surface of things.
Would not be too curious about my past.
Must understand anticipation.
Must have an imagination.
Must be able to put up with my *shit*.
Must be able to kiss for a long time.

and couldn't think of anything else.

Susan drove back to the house after visiting her grandfather. She walked along the hall and into the bright pocket of the kitchen.

Outside, in the twilight, Cliff and Jade wandered through the wilderness of the backyard. Susan watched them from the kitchen, intrigued. Cliff had black bruises on his chest and purple crescents of broken skin on his back and it took a slow moment before she realised what had caused them.

Jade was pale and slight compared to him. They were combing through the old garden, pulling off leaves from likely looking plants and smelling them. Jade tasted everything. Susan sat on a chair in the kitchen and watched them.

Daniel explored one of the old farm sheds. Along the wall were boxes and boxes of metal: machinery parts, nuts, bolts, tools, chains, sheets of metal and tin, iron bars lying around the floor, ball-bearings, busted bikes, dismembered cars. A newer car that Cliff seemed to be working on; parts glistening with oil arrayed around it.

Hanging on the walls were all sorts of odds and ends, wire,

string, metal containers, knives and pots. Old food tins: flour, sugar, tea, tobacco. There was a sign hanging on the wall: 'Keep away from this or you'll bugger it up!' There was a bed coated with mildew and mould. He held his nose. He walked further into the shed. There was a box under a blanket under a table. He pulled the handle and it slid out. Something exploded with claws and hissing. He jumped back and the thing's rasping furious noise filled the shed. Daniel watched the goanna's tail disappear into the long grass.

His laugh turned into a dust-coated cough. He opened the lid of the box and it was filled with more interesting junk. He went through it and then walked back to the yard.

'There's some great stuff in the shed, Cliff. You could weld it together, make sculptures.'

'What?'

'Make things out of it. You know, sculptures, figures, stuff like that, to sell.'

Cliff looked at him, his face empty.

'Just an idea,' Daniel said.

Daniel squatted and ran his hands through the damp earth. The light seeping through the clouds was yellow and made their skins look odd. The clouds looked as if someone had tried to stretch them out with a rake but given it up as a bad joke. He watched Cliff and Jade pushing and shoving each other like kids, their bodies blackened by shadow. As he watched them turn their skin changed from black to gold.

Jade was laughing. She looked at him and he pretended his eyes were somewhere else. Her back was criss-crossed by the tight material of her top as if her bones were loose and floating inside her and in need of a sling.

They rinsed dirt off their arms and legs. Suddenly Cliff had the hose and sprang about with it like a loony fireman. Jade screamed and that surprised Daniel so much that he forgot to move. Cliff nailed him in the back. The water, colder than he thought it would be, drenched his shirt and slipped down into his pants.

Cliff chased Jade but she had found a bucket somewhere and was searching for a tap to fill it. The hose reached its limit. Curly barked at Cliff. Cliff kinked the hose and Curly camped at the tap and tried to drink the water leaking and spraying from it; snapping at it with his yellow dog teeth as if it were alive.

Jade found the tap near the fence and filled her bucket; then doubled back around the other side of the house. Daniel backed out of range and saw Susan watching them from the kitchen. Jade crept along the wall behind Cliff.

She was nearly there; if she had just popped around as Cliff checked the other direction she would have been okay. Curly was still barking. Jade stared at Daniel with her palm upraised in a plea for some kind of help. Cliff turned the other way and Daniel nodded and Jade came dashing around the corner of the house.

Daniel saw Cliff turn and tried to shout a warning but he was too late. It happened too quickly. Jade swung the bucket but most of the water missed Cliff and landed on Curly, who yelped in surprise and trotted off to shake his coat. Cliff grabbed Jade and held her across the chest and stuck the hose down her shorts and put the bucket on her head and tapped on it with his knuckles. Daniel laughed nervously. Jade was squealing, the sound muffled and strange under the bucket. Cliff tapped it hard with the hose and Jade struggled fiercely to break his grip. Cliff laughed his stupid laugh.

'Give up?' he yelled at her.

'Give up?' she yelled back.

They held each other until Jade went limp and only then did Cliff let her go. He went to the tap and turned it off, still laughing.

Jade tore the bucket off her head and looked around. She

was breathing hard and her eyes were wild. She was drenched and her hair clung to her face. She had red marks on her arms and neck.

Daniel plucked a cigarette from the packet on the step and lit it and said nothing.

Cliff wound up the hose.

'You shit!' she said.

She walked over to the garden. Daniel could hear her wet clothes slapping against her skin. She picked up a handful of the mud their feet had churned up. Daniel shook his head when he realised what she was going to do.

She threw the mud, put her back into it so it collapsed in mid-air and spread out and slapped into Cliff's back and caught in his hair, splattered over his bare back. Cliff turned and made for Jade, and Daniel stood up reflexively. Jade stood for a moment as if she couldn't move, stuck to the ground in a dream, but then she ran screaming into the house with Cliff close behind her, mud sliding off him onto the floor.

Susan yelled at them both then looked at Daniel, who shrugged his shoulders.

He could hear them bumping around inside, her shrieking and his roaring. A train rolled by on the tracks down the hill and he watched it and the dark silhouettes at each window.

Inside, Jade grasped at Cliff's body, pressed her face against his whiskers and long red tongue. All Cliff could think about was dirt. Dirt and blood; mixing together in a dark whirlpool.

Daniel threw the cigarette onto the grass and went into the kitchen.

'They seem to like each other,' he said to Susan.

'Yes. They seem to be on the same level.'

'Don't you approve?'

'It's not that I do or don't approve, I just can't see anything coming from it. Cliff needs to settle down. He's still as wild as he was years ago.'

'I suppose so. But at least he's happy now.'

'But for how long?'

Daniel shrugged again. He lowered his voice.

'I think she may be the first.'

'The first what?'

'His first lover,' he whispered.

'Really? Why would you say that?'

'I don't know. It's just a feeling. Maybe it's because he's one of the shyest people I've ever met.'

'I've never thought of Cliff as shy.'

'No?'

Susan shook her head.

Daniel filled the sink with hot water and detergent and began to wash the dishes piled up on the bench. He tried to think of something to say.

'Do you like cooking?' he asked her.

'I don't mind it, although I hate cooking a nice meal and having people wolf it down in two seconds flat.'

'I think I know who you're talking about.'

'Can you cook?'

'Yep. I'll cook tonight.'

'That would be nice. Do you think we should ask the other two to do their share?'

'Not if you value your life!'

She laughed.

'You've got a nice laugh,' he said.

'Thank you.'

He could hear an owl hooting outside; not regularly but every now and then. He wondered how it decided when to hoot and when not to. He finished the dishes and was surprised to find the kitchen empty when he turned around. He looked through the cupboards for ingredients and started to make dinner. After an hour Susan reappeared in the kitchen.

'The food's nearly ready. Do you think it's safe to interrupt them yet?'

'Well, if they want to eat, they're going to have to stop whatever they're doing. Want me to see?'

'Do you mind?'

'No.'

Susan went up the hall. There was no sound from behind Cliff's door. She knocked softly.

'Food,' she said, and walked away.

Cliff and Jade emerged sooner than Daniel expected, still damp and bedraggled.

Susan told them they'd both have to clean up before they could eat anything and they both looked at her wide-eyed and then darted into the bathroom. They could hear water splashing on the floor and more squealing.

'Any excuse,' said Daniel.

'We're never going to eat,' sighed Susan.

Eventually they emerged, more or less clean, and sat down.

Susan carried the pot of steaming spaghetti to the table.

They ate and Daniel watched the others over his fork. They talked about nothing until they were all laughing at nothing together and trying to chew at the same time. Everyone except Susan drank beer. They ate until they were full and then tucked into ice-cream.

They heard a noise from the cupboard and Cliff searched inside with his hand and pulled out a mousetrap, complete with a mouse broken nearly in two; its eyes bugging out of its head but not yet dead. He bent back the trap's spring, grabbed the mouse's tail and flung it toward the closed kitchen window before anyone could say anything.

The mouse hit the glass with a wet slap and slid down onto the windowsill.

Daniel laughed as hard as he could ever remember laughing. He hung his head and tried to stop but when he looked up Cliff still hadn't moved, was still looking at the mouse quivering on the sill. That made Daniel laugh even harder. Even Susan's face was red and tears shone on her face. Jade was on the floor.

Daniel noticed Cliff's neck was red but then he turned to them, straight-faced until his features split in a foolish gap-toothed, gold-capped grin.

And that set them off again.

Cliff leaned over the sink and opened the window, plucked up the mouse by its tail, and threw it out onto the grass.

'Something'll get it. A snake or a goanna,' he said.

His comment didn't help the others regain their composure.

Later, they sat and drank coffee on the verandah. Cliff was quiet. Jade kept giggling. They could hear a jet ploughing through the sky but couldn't see it.

Susan brought out cake. The others crammed theirs into their mouths until there was none left except for Susan's piece on the plate beside her chair. Jade eyed the piece but Susan seemed not to notice.

Daniel relaxed and witty comments came out loose and flying. Whatever had been hanging over him, dry and black, seemed to have vanished for the time being.

Somehow the conversation turned to bellybuttons and soon everyone except Susan stood, pulled up their shirts, and compared.

'No one's seeing my bellybutton,' said Susan.

They laughed at her sitting there, sipping tea, cocking an eyebrow at them, refusing to reveal her bellybutton.

Cliff told them about the golden steam train that was supposed to haunt the hills.

'Our great-grandfather used to sit out here and wait for it to appear.'

'Did he ever see it?'

'No, but my grandmother said she once saw a man covered in coal dust in the kitchen. She came in from the garden, saw this black man standing there. Just standing. She said she could see right through him, he had his lights on, she said, fire running through him, smoke curling off his head. She was a bit mad though.'

'Oh, she wasn't, Cliff,' said Susan.

'Yes she was, she was off her rocker!'

'Who broke the mirror?' asked Jade, out of the blue.

The others looked at her.

'What mirror?'

'The nice one in the bathroom.'

'I broke it,' said Cliff, but the others didn't hear him.

'Oh, Cliff broke it,' said Susan, 'ages ago, with his head, when he was little. We came up to visit our grandparents. They used to live here. Cliff was bouncing on the bed, and he bounced off and hit his head against it. He didn't hurt himself though.'

'I don't remember doing it,' said Cliff.

'Oh, poor thing,' said Jade.

'And my grandmother couldn't stand me after that. She thought I was evil.'

'She didn't think you were evil, Cliff,' said Susan tightly.

'She did a good impression of it.'

Cliff smiled and Jade stared at him and Susan with equal interest. No one said anything for a moment. Daniel could see Jade's curiosity ticking over.

'I thought your grandparents brought you up,' she said.

'This was before. This was before our parents were killed and before my father disappeared.'

'Sorry?'

'Cliff is my half-brother. Didn't he tell you?'
'No.'

They sat a little longer and then Susan stretched, pointing her fingers at the ceiling, and yawned. Her eyetooth was discoloured like a drop of vanilla in milk. The muscles in her back slid against each other under her shirt. Daniel thought the yawn was fake through and through.

'I'm tired,' she said.

'Aren't you going to eat your cake?' said Jade brightly.

'Mmmm, yes, thanks for reminding me.'

She picked up the piece and ate it.

'Goodnight.'

'Goodnight.'

Daniel looked at his watch. Midnight. The fig tree swayed and creaked in the breeze like old machinery. Moonlight glazed the leaves.

'It's a great tree,' said Daniel.

'Yeah.'

'What's the time, Daniel?' said Jade.

'Twelve.'

'Why don't you wear a watch?' Cliff asked her.

'They stop working near me. They always have.'

'Bullshit.'

'No bullshit.'

She undid his watchband and slid Cliff's chunky watch off his arm and onto hers.

'Wait and see,' she said and slid off his lap and disappeared into the house without another word. Daniel closed his eyes and listened to the sound of her bare feet on the boards as she walked the length of the house. The sound belonged somewhere else but he couldn't place it and didn't want to.

'He said it was a special tree,' Cliff said. 'Magic. He said my great-grandfather planted it so the cows could find their way home in the dark. So they always knew where they were.'

'Who said?'

'My grandfather. Stupid old bugger.'

'You never did like him.'

'They didn't like me. Never did,' said Cliff. 'I'm not making it up. They thought my father had something to do with Susan's father going walkabout.

'Did he?'

'I don't know. Probably.'

He smiled.

'Seriously?'

'How should I know? I wasn't born you wanker!'

'I thought you might know.'

'Nup.'

'Hey, I wanted to ask you. How come Jade came with us the other night, I thought you didn't know her?'

'I didn't. When that prick hit you, you went down. When I hit him back and grabbed you, she was hanging on to us.'

'Nothing to it,' he said, shrugged his shoulders, and followed Jade into the house.

The other one loved the river. I'd see her sometimes along the bank. It's where she thought about things, maybe, later, where she sat and wrote her letters to me. She sent them to me care of the railway when I was out doing the tracks. She always seemed to know where I was; I don't know how. I'd read them by the light of the fire, the night stretching out dry and inky black all round; then watch them curl into ash as I stretched out on the ground. The smoke, faint with perfume, made sleepy men rise and stare into the dark.

Dumb buggers the lot.

Roy stood in his flat with a heavy head and listened to the morning birds sing to each other. He went into the bathroom, slipped a fresh blade into his razor and slowly and carefully shaved his face. The fluorescent tube exposed the years etched into his skin, the blue veins throbbing near his temples. He wet his hair and combed it neatly across his skull. He rubbed on aftershave, its smell like a solid presence in the bathroom, in the mirror.

He had not seen Jade for days.

He felt better on the outside, clearer. The blade did its work. He sat at the top of the stairs and listened for signs of life in the town. He sucked in the cool morning air and felt it slide around his lungs and creep in behind his eyes. Mist spilled from the river and he watched it float and turn in the space over the street.

He dipped his feet into slippers and set off to the newsagent. When he arrived he pulled a paper from the bundle on the footpath and left money on the shop step. He walked back to his own shop, unlocked the door and stepped inside. He ran his eyes over the honeycomb of heating and filtration equipment behind the tanks. Everything seemed to be in order. He moved steadily along the tank racks feeding the fish and periodically wiping humidity from the back of his neck with a handkerchief.

Michael reached another town as night fell. He walked quickly through its streets and slipped down to the river and rested his back against the concrete of the bridge that spanned it. Exhausted, he listened to the water with closed eyes and then folded himself into the dry earth and became, under the moon's light, as black and as solid as coal.

Saturday.

The new day's light through Daniel's window was obscured by climbing vines which swayed in the breeze and loaded the room with invisible perfume. He could hear the world calling instructions to itself. A spider had built a web across the window and was wrapping an insect in silk.

He bumped his head against the door as he opened it. Things still seemed further away than they were. He went to the bathroom and winced again when he saw the side of his face in the mirror. He took some deep breaths. He showered and breathed in the pure clean steam, forcing it in and out of his lungs in hot clouds, daring the pain to crack his side.

But it didn't.

He washed his body carefully; soaping his ears until they burned cleanly. He checked his face for spots and wrinkles. He thought the bruise looked a bit sexy.

There was a heady smell of powder and perfume in the bathroom. A small black mark caught his eye and he leant closer and looked; a single sea-shell curl of lash; coal black and abandoned on the creamy porcelain.

He dressed quickly and drove down to Greenhill to telephone his father. The streets were quiet.

'Dad, it's Daniel.'

'Where the hell have you been?'

'Sorry Dad. I've been staying with a friend in Greenhill. I'll be back in a few days, okay? And I don't think I want to keep working for you.'

Daniel said it all as quickly as he could. He thought it didn't sound too bad.

'Yeah, okay, that's fine son.'

His father sounded almost reasonable.

'Listen, a friend of yours has been ringing here trying to find you. There's some bad news. If you'd have called earlier . . . well . . .'

'What news? Who rang?'

'Your friend Sylvia died a few weeks ago. Something about an overdose. I'm sorry, mate.'

Daniel stared hard at the glass in the telephone booth. He hung up and stepped out onto the concrete of the footpath. His legs were jelly. He sat down on the kerb and hung his head. He sat for a long time. A few tears squeezed out onto his cheeks. People drove by and stared at him. Soon, morning shoppers filled the street. When a car parked in front of him, close enough to reach out and touch, he stood, found his car and drove back to the house.

Susan scratched. Mosquitoes had bitten her during the night and the lumps burned and itched on her face and she had to concentrate to not scratch them. There was one next to her mouth and one in the soft skin behind her knee. The sun made the air in the room as warm and heavy as melted butter. She remembered her grandmother's mosquito net and wondered where it was.

After a shower and breakfast she went and started to go through her grandparents' belongings. Dust flew and she sneezed and blew her nose with pink tissues. There was no sign of life from the others and she was thankful for the peace.

The boxes had been packed years ago. Each box seemed to hold a single class of relic. She pulled out yellowing clothes and laid them in a pile on the floor. She found her mother's wedding dress; as tiny and frail as a chrysalis. Then her grandmother's wedding dress. Tiny children's clothes. She stared long and hard at her mother's dress. She was tempted to try it on. She went into the hall and held it up against herself and looked at her image in the mirror. She stood there for a long time then, finally, folded up the dress and put it back in the box.

She heard a knock on the door and the sound of it jarred her from her contemplation. She listened.

'Yoo hoo, missus!'

A man's voice. She wondered where everyone else was. She stood and slapped the dust from her hands and went to answer the door.

She could not see the man clearly, just his silhouette on the step. She could see he wore a baggy hat and was carrying a box in his arms. As she moved closer she saw his beard and the two bars of white floating in it. His clothes were dirty and a whiff of unwashed flesh bothered her nose. He was smaller than he had seemed ten paces back and he gave her a toothy grin as she stopped at the door and said, 'Yes?'

'Morning missus. Would you like some honey? Very cheap. Best quality.'

She was slightly amused and she had to think for a moment before the question sank through. She took a deep breath and reminded herself she was in the country. He was already taking jars from the box he carried and holding them up to the light.

'Brushbox, beeauutiful! Ironbark. Clover.'

She could not help smiling at his little performance.

'No thanks. Not today.'

Disappointment oozed from him and his smile faded.

'You sure?'

'Yes, quite sure, thank you.'

'No sweet toof's inside?'

'No.'

'Oh well, I'll come back some other time. You might want some then.'

He didn't sound as disappointed as he looked. He turned and trotted back down the steps and she watched him load the honey into the back of a rusted truck and drive off in a cloud of blue smoke.

What a strange man, she thought, and went back inside.

She started on another box. Letters mainly and mostly addressed to her mother and grandmother. A few rare letters between her father and mother. She had read a few before but others were new and she read them in a whisper, moving her lips and breathing sound into the words. She searched for her grandfather's distinctive hand but found nothing in it. Letters piled up on the floor. Her knees popped as she stood. She bent and opened the flap of the next box. It was filled with all sorts of odds and ends and she groaned. Something curved and drab caught her eye among the artificial angles and she reached in and took hold of it. It was cool to the touch and almost soft. Wood. Something jumped inside her and she pulled the object out of the box forcefully and sent things bouncing and clanging onto the floor. It was a box, as wide as her hand, made entirely from grey driftwood. Her grand-father had made it for her long ago and she had kept her secret—her special—things, in it. She thought it had been lost years ago.

She fumbled with the tiny catch but her fingernails got in the way and she swore at them and vowed to cut them off. She went into the kitchen and Daniel was standing in the doorway. He watched her and made no move to leave. She was annoyed.

'Hello,' he said.

'Hi,' she said curtly.

She plucked a knife from the drawer and wedged it between the catch and the wood and jiggled the knife until the steel separated and the lid swung open with a scrape. Daniel watched her as she lay the box on the shelf and held its contents up to the light.

Half a seashell, carefully sawn to reveal its helical architec-ture, its worn creamy surface glowing pink and blue. A bright copper penny with a hole drilled through its kangaroo-heart centre. A piece of blue glass, its edges rounded and polished by the sea.

Susan returned the things to the box and took it into her room. Daniel watched her go and then, he too, went into his room and shut the door. He lay down on the mattress and cradled his head in the pillow, shutting out as much sound as he could, wrapping the huge quiet like a bandage around him.

Cliff was dreaming, flying lickety-split and low over the town. The air was clear and he could see for miles and miles. He could feel something swinging underneath him, something attached, embedded deep in his gut. He had to stay high but he could still see, that was the best thing. His eyes were ordinary no more but sprang out of his head, heavy with added metal and glass. He spun the cold brass with his hands and kept things focused. His hands moved too fast to see but he could see every leaf on every tree, every blade of grass, fish swimming far below the surface of the sea, the river. He saw people out and about and they were more interesting than ordinary people. He watched them in their houses, through glowing windows, floating. The hair of a boy a precise shade of gold as he leant into a ray of light and kissed a dark-haired girl.

He woke and Jade was sprawled over him and the room was warm.

She was awake and watching him.

She teased him.

'I love sex, don't you?'

'It's okay,' he said, red-cheeked. He didn't want to know. He couldn't bear to think of her with other men. It made him feel ill.

'Where were you born?' he asked her.

'I was born on an ocean liner while my parents were cruising the world. Prematurely,' she added.

'Were not.'

'Were so. I was blue when I was born. The cord was wrapped around my neck.'

'Why is your name Jade?'

She pulled a tiny green figure from the midst of everything else that hung around her neck.

'Dad said it was his good-luck charm. He said it saved his life. So he named me Jade when I was born and gave it to me.'

'What if you'd been a boy?'

'I guess my name wouldn't be Jade, would it?'

'What happened to your mother?'

'She lives in Paris.'

'Have you been to see her?'

'No.'

'Can you do this?' she said, and put her leg straight up into the air, curled up her trunk and touched the leg behind her knee with her tongue.

'I wouldn't *want* to do that,' he said.

'Can you kiss your elbow?' she whispered. 'If you can you're a fairy.'

He tried hard, bending his shoulder past safety. Then he tried the other and failed as well.

'Sorry, you're not a fairy.'

'It's bloody stupid anyway.'

'You're bloody stupid!'

Cliff put on his clothes and left the room. He went looking for Daniel and found him.

'Come on. Get up, the day's nearly over!'

Daniel rolled over and looked at him.

'Come on, come and have a drink with me.'

He left the room and Daniel, after a while, pulled himself up and followed him.

They sat on the back step in the shade and drank. Soon, Jade came and sat down with them. Daniel sipped his beer and said nothing to either of them. Cliff teased Curly with a stick. Jade got up and left, disgusted with something.

'Have you seen Susan?' asked Cliff.

'Yeah, I saw her a while ago.'

Cliff went inside and knocked on Susan's door.

'Come and have a drink with us,' he said.

'Maybe later.'

Daniel drank as quickly as he could. He didn't feel any better. The day, despite its simple beauty, seemed drained of possibility; as fragile and shaky as a sick lover. He stood up and discovered he couldn't walk straight. Curly barked at him.

Cliff came back and they drank more beer until Daniel was past caring.

Cliff jumped up on a box, clowned around, starting telling all the jokes he knew in a booming voice that sounded strange rolling over the quiet countryside. Jade appeared from somewhere to watch him. He was good, Daniel thought, he *was* a clown. Daniel fell and rolled in the warm green grass. Cliff cartwheeled and somersaulted and then collapsed, panting, his floppy hat in front of his eyes. He picked up clods of earth and juggled them. He had tried to teach Daniel once. 'Try it when you're drunk,' he had said, 'you need to feel loose, not think about what your hands are doing.' Cliff stood with a cigarette in his mouth and spun the clods until they broke. Daniel was thoroughly impressed.

Cliff disappeared into the shed.

Daniel heard the hiss and crack of the welder. He followed Cliff and found him swaying next to the car, face masked, welding steel onto the roof. The paint burning off the car filled the shed with noxious-smelling smoke.

'What the fuck are you doing, Cliff?'

'Like you said. Seen that movie *Chitty Chitty Bang Bang*?'

'Yeah.'

'I'm making a flying, floating car.'

Daniel watched the welder spit and shielded his eyes against the white light. Cliff stopped and scrambled through the junk for the right sized pieces to weld to the car. Daniel went looking too. When they had finished the car looked as dangerous as a fishhook. Fractured metal broke from the skin of the car like bones. It was too gruesome.

'I love it,' said Daniel.

When he closed his eyes Daniel could see a blue spot. He was pleased. When he closed his eyes he couldn't see Sylvia any more.

Cliff lost interest in the car and went to find Jade. Daniel stepped back into the sun. Someone's washing was on the line, pushed gently around by the breeze. He lay on his back in the grass and stared up. Shorts, tops, dresses, and underwear floated above him. They changed shape as he watched. The underwear, the beautiful snowy underwear, became cherubs, swans, powdered scalps. He pushed himself deeper into the backyard grass. Insects crawled over him. Clouds stood like bricks in the sky. He set his head into the sun and felt the scalding delicious touch of it. He opened his eyes and everything was tinged blue; his skin was silver, edged with gold. Underneath, at the bottom of everything, after the alcohol had burned away anything coherent, he was surprised to find, not pain, not anger, but something calm, something approaching relief. It was like a kiss forgotten, remembered.

Susan lay on her bed. One set of fingers was hooked into the sheet and the other toyed with the shell, coin and glass. Her room was a cube of warm air and she was half-asleep. She had woken from a dream and was trying desperately to return to it. She had seen a man whose face kept changing—that was when she could see his face—but her pleasure as she watched him had remained constant. She opened her eyes. She closed her eyes. He appeared at the end of the bed, looking down at her. The strength of his image startled her.

He wasn't the same as before. She watched as he moved around the room. He stood behind the door and she held her breath as his skin changed from its smoky base to a dark varnished chocolate. He shifted to green as he stepped in front of the wall, then blue and yellow as he moved along the bed, past the windows. For an instant she saw through him as he stood and touched the glass and a rainbow sparkled from him and spilled for a second on her leg, warm red through cool blue. He walked toward her and his eyes were steady and his white teeth split his face smiling and he reached down and touched her with his hand. He touched her, slid his arm along her leg and she reached out and felt layers of muscle under his skin like metal under oil.

Much too hard, she thought, opening her eyes.

The room was bright and a breeze pushed against the curtains and her heart was quick and she laughed aloud.

Late in the night Jade woke to a strange noise in the house. She listened and then worked out what it was. She rose from the bed, opened the door and walked towards the sound. Someone was vomiting in the bathroom. She heard violent retching and then a thin moan. She pushed open the door and looked into the room. It was Daniel. He was kneeling in front of the toilet in his underpants. She could see the muscles in his back tense as he retched again. She turned and stepped into the kitchen and filled a glass with water. She stood outside the door and waited until she heard him rinse his mouth over the sink then pushed open the door and offered him the water. He said nothing but took the water and drank a mouthful, waited a moment, then drank the rest. She took the glass from his hand and refilled it and he drank that too.

'Thanks,' he croaked.

She watched him walk, bent over like an old man, back to his room; then she went back to bed herself.

I'm standing on the jetty that stood at the bottom of the hill. Just standing, breathing, watching the water, the sun on the water disappearing into it like the thickest piece of green glass. Hot. Bloody hot. We had been there all afternoon. Putting on a show for the families in the park on the other side of the river, under the big trees. Extra application when a girl was watching. I felt sorry for them having to watch. As the sun set everyone went home but I stayed out on the jetty. Haze out to sea as if there were bushfires burning way over the horizon. Fire jumping between swells as if they were trees.

I remember my pride at how young and strong I was, how hard I was from work and how brown from the sun.

I remember the river when I remember the war. I remember lying in a field behind the lines. Wounded. Wounded. Gas in the eyes and throat was like breathing kerosene. Enough to be useless. Sinking into the long grass was better than the softest bed. The sun came out and warmed us and we lay quiet in the field and some smoked cigarettes. I remember the ringing in my ears and lying still so my eyes didn't hurt too much. The lads uneasy out in the open. They could still hear the rumbling of the guns like a storm.

I remember the ripping sound of my own skin and flesh. The sizzle of hot metal through my skin, scratching and burning and wet. I opened my shirt and surprise! surprise! there was my old body, the one from the riverbank back home, the one I had been so proud of, white as chalk under the grime and creased with scarlet.

Sunday morning.

Jade turned on the gas to boil water and then bent double as a cramp hit her. The gas hissed out and she struck the match anyway and the gas ballooned into flame that rushed and singed her hair. She took a step backwards and tripped

and fell over Curly's bowl, cracking her head on the floor.
Dog biscuits flew across the room.

Susan hurried down the hall bleary eyed and smelt the gas.
She saw Jade lying on the floor and her face slid from surprise
to concern. She peeled hair out of her eyes and bent over
Jade's body.

'Are you all right? What happened?'

Jade's head swam and she said nothing.

Susan ran to the bathroom and got a washer and ran it
under cold water and came back and dabbed it on Jade's
cheeks and forehead.

Jade grinned.

'What happened?'

'I had an accident with the gas.'

'Can you get up? Can I get you some water?'

'No, I think I'm okay.' Susan helped her to her feet and
into a chair.

'I was making tea. Do you want a cup?' asked Jade.

'Don't be silly; I'll make it. Are you sure you're okay?'

'Yeah.'

They sat at the kitchen table and sipped tea. Jade held her
chin in her hand and grimaced.

'What's the matter?'

'Cramps.'

'Oh. Bad?'

'Yeah.'

'A hot-water bottle helps.'

'Do we have one?'

'Well . . . somewhere.'

'It doesn't matter.'

'Walking sometimes helps, some kind of exercise.'

'Where would I walk to?'

'Up to the creek? I could come with you.'

'Okay.'

They dressed quickly and set off up the slope. Curly followed them. Susan's mind went blank.

Soon they reached the pool with the waterfall and stopped at the edge and recovered their breath. Crows perched in trees and complained about everything.

'Going in?' said Jade.

'No, I don't think I will.'

Jade undressed down to her knickers and stepped over to the edge of the rock.

'Is it deep enough to jump in here?'

'Yes.'

Jade jumped in, swam around. She pulled herself out onto the rocks underneath the ledge and began to climb. Susan thought she looked half-starved; her ribs and the bones in her neck pressing hard against her skin. She reached the ledge and turned around and shouted something but it was lost in the roar of the waterfall.

'What?' asked Susan, but Jade had already jumped, pushing off with all her strength and sailing through the air with a grin from ear to ear, arms and legs flailing. She hit the water and disappeared and Susan watched the water hide all trace of her until her head, black with water, broke the surface. Susan smiled.

Jade pulled herself out and came and sat near Susan on a sunny rock.

'Should have brought a towel.'

'It's okay, I'll dry off in the sun.'

Susan's stomach rumbled and she pictured chocolate and cheesecake. The sun threw light over the tops of trees like a net. Spray from the waterfall drifted through the air like clear pearls of nothing.

'He likes you, you know,' said Jade.

'Who?'

'Daniel.'

'Do you think so?'

'Yeah.'

'I think Daniel is a bit too much like Cliff for my liking.'

'No, Daniel's nothing like Cliff. I think he's sad about something. That's why he drank so much yesterday.'

They paused. Even though Susan had questions for Jade she didn't ask them. She didn't really want to know the answers.

'Cliff said you were married?'

'Yes.'

'Where's your husband?'

'He's at home.'

'Aren't you getting on?'

'Something like that . . . do you think Daniel knows I'm married?'

'I don't know. It wouldn't make any difference. Anyway, maybe I'm wrong.'

'It's hard to tell with men sometimes,' said Susan. 'Anyway I'm finished with all that business, I've made enough mistakes to last me for a while.'

'I'd root him,' said Jade. She leaned to one side and farted. 'Excuse me,' she said. 'Anyway, just don't start anything you can't finish. That's what my grandmother always said to me.'

With that, Jade scrambled into her clothes and headed back down the trail. Susan shook her head in amusement and followed.

Daniel lay awake in his room. The skin on his arms, legs and neck had erupted in angry red marks that itched and burnt. He thought it was his skin reacting to the grass; it had always been sensitive. His head pounded and he kept still. The skin on his face was burnt from the sun like a blush gone horribly wrong. He ventured out into the kitchen to drink but saw no one. In the bathroom he eyed the broken mirror and then carried it back to his room and propped it up beside the bed. It sat and watched him like a huge silver eye at a keyhole and he watched his reflection and made sure he didn't fade away. He thought about Sylvia. He was surprised to find he had no curiosity about how her death had occurred. He tried to imagine heaven and hell. It struck him that he knew things about her life that her family would never know and would never want to. Things he would remember until they faded from his memory or he died. The thought made him anxious. He wanted to tell someone—confess it all—but there was no one to tell.

He remembered her in sharp detail then couldn't remember her at all. He kept seeing her face on the day he had surprised her with her lover. For a sickening, intoxicating moment, he was glad that *she* was dead and that he was still alive.

He was disgusted with himself.

In the steady dark of the room the shadows moved. He dozed between itching.

He saw a wedding day. Panic as he looked down and saw a dress. A soft little girl's body connected to his mind and as frightening as any monster in a cupboard. Then excitement as a green-eyed young girl appeared. My best friend, he thought. And then an even younger boy with thin brown arms and legs, wild brown hair and rotten smiling teeth. They helped him climb a drainpipe on the side of an old house. Stifling giggles, they helped each other onto a wide verandah. They peeked wide-eyed through windows. Inside, a bride and groom sat trapped by one another on a dark and dusty sofa. A clock ticked, clouds cut the sun and turned the room dim and private. Sounds were captured between walls, underneath the sky, between here and there.

They curved and breathed around each other. Any sound

they made was swallowed by the house but he could still hear birds singing outside, sweeter than he had ever heard. Must be my little girl ears, he thought. Neighbours called to each other and laughed. Cars in the street. Music like mist, without a beginning or an end.

He watched; frozen. His best friend giggled. The small boy giggled.

'Shut up, I want to hear what they're saying.'

'Why?'

'Just shut up!'

They were intent on each other. The man seemed to be holding her up and together, his thick fingers sinking into her skin. He could see his eyes boring into her, dark and intense. She was bending and swaying as if she were soft at the core and had bones of rubber. Then he was through the window or through the wall and standing there in the room with them but they were oblivious and that annoyed him more than anything. He breathed in air as thick as water and shouted at them but what came out was a little girl's squeal. No reaction. He waved his little pink girl hands in front of their faces but he seemed to be invisible to them.

He opened his eyes. The room had not changed. His reflection in the mirror had not changed, but, lying there, he felt different; as if something had penetrated his flesh and hardened, gleaming, just under the skin.

Susan looked at her watch. She decided to ask Cliff again if he would come with her to the hospital.

She knocked on his door.

'Come in.'

Jade was lying naked on the bed watching television, propped up with pillows like a hospital patient. She smoked a cigarette and tapped the ash into a glass ashtray riding on the swell of her breastbone. There was an empty glass beside her with a spoon in it and what looked like the last of the ice-cream around her mouth. Susan was surprised that Jade didn't seem to care who was at the door; just kept on watching television and then turned her head and smiled.

'Hello.'

'Do you know where Cliff is?'

'He's out the back I think.'

Susan looked for Cliff and found him and he looked at her with blank surprise when she told him where she was going.

'No, I'm not coming. No point. There's no use, he can't hear you,' he said.

'I think he can. The doctor told me he won't last much longer.'

'They said that years ago.'

'Well, this time I think they're right.'

Cliff bent over the car.

'If you don't come now you might not be able to say goodbye to him.'

'I said goodbye to him years ago.'

Susan bit her tongue and turned and walked away.

'Hey, can you bring back something to eat?'

Susan stormed off, her ears burning. When she went into the kitchen Daniel was sitting at the table. His hair was wet and slick and he smelt of powder.

'Do *you* want to come with me to see my grandfather?'

'Sorry?' he said, and she wanted to wring his neck, wanted to wring all their necks.

'You heard me.'

'Sure,' he said, 'okay.' And that was that. They climbed into the car and Susan drove too fast into town.

Clack, clack, clack. Daniel listened to her heels on the floor. He could have followed her with his eyes closed but instead he watched her from the safety of his slower step.

'Are your grandparents still alive?' she asked briskly.

'Two of them.'

'You're lucky,' she said. 'He's down the end.'

The corridor ran the length of the hospital wing and was breached along its length by rooms brimful of aged men. Susan talked to the nurse.

His eyes were closed when they stepped into the ward and the afternoon light etched a maze of lines into his face. His body was slipping off his bones. His skull hovered underneath his skin and pushed it out like a tent. Susan bent and spoke over the bed, rubbed the bony hand and held it against her lips, her cheek.

Uncomfortable, Daniel looked away.

A woman sat with the man in the bed across the room. He listened to their shouted conversation.

'Mr Pike, I'm Elizabeth. I'm the social worker replacing Margaret.'

'What?'

'I'm Elizabeth. I'm the social worker replacing Margaret.'

'Social worker? I've already got one; Margaret, I don't need another one.'

'Yes, I'm *replacing her*!'

'She's good, Margaret. Do anything for you.'

'Yes.'

'She got married, you know.'

'Yes.'

'Got married and moved south. I wonder where her replacement's got to?'

Daniel tried not to laugh. He sat and watched Susan and her grandfather. She seemed to have forgotten about him sitting there. He walked over to the window and looked out. The hospital had a good view across the town. He sat up on the sill.

Soon he heard someone singing. It was only a whisper but he knew it was Susan. She pushed the words out flat but the tune curled up their ends like dry paper and sent them floating around on the room's imperceptible currents. Daniel strained to catch the words but could only hear their music. He knew if he turned around she would probably stop so he kept looking out the window until, when he closed his eyes and opened them again, he could tell what had changed and what had stayed the same.

They sat for another hour.

'Maybe Cliff is right,' said Susan. 'Maybe he can't hear me.'

They left the hospital. Daniel looked at each face in each bed as they walked out. A man with half his face missing waved and half-smiled. Daniel tried to smile back.

On their way to the house they stopped at the milk bar and bought fish and chips. The smell of food brought Cliff and Jade running as they walked through the door. They sat down and ate.

'There're bones in this fish,' said Jade.

'Sorry,' said Daniel, insincerely.

Cliff sucked the flesh from the bones with loose smacking lips. He stacked them on the table near his plate.

'You're a grub, Cliff,' Daniel said.

He pictured some huge beast giving Cliff's body the same treatment. He chuckled stupidly and a bone caught in his throat and he threw back his head and gave a strangled cough. His head began to spin with blood. Susan stared at him. Jade jumped from her chair as quick as a flash and thumped Daniel so hard on the back he half-expected to see the bone jutting from his lip, but the white sliver shot out like a tiny boomerang and landed near the salt shaker.

'Thanks,' Daniel croaked, when he got his breath back.

'That's okay,' she said, and sat down again, still chewing.

Cliff looked at him and laughed.

Susan excused herself and went to her room. Cliff and Jade went into the lounge and turned on the television. Daniel followed. He felt very tired. He was thinking of funerals and weddings.

They watched television and didn't speak to one another. The movie finished. Jade persuaded Cliff to rub her shoulders. Daniel watched his thick hairy fingers move across her back.

Jade yelped and scolded.

Cliff stopped what he was doing and walked from the room. The television droned on. Minutes passed and Cliff did not return. Jade shifted across and sat in front of Daniel.

'Come on, keep going. Remember that I saved your life before.'

'I don't think Cliff would like it.'

'Don't worry about him. Come on, you owe me!'

Daniel, reluctantly, put his hands onto her back and copied the movements Cliff had made. Her skin was smooth and warm and impossibly pleasant against his fingers. He relaxed slightly and began to feel for the hard, tense muscles in her shoulders and neck. She drew in her breath but said nothing. She directed his hands. He could smell her perfume and her hair.

'Careful!' she said.

'Sorry.'

'Your hands are much softer than Cliff's.'

His soft hands began to ache and he screwed up his face. He couldn't feel her any more, the tips of his fingers were nearly numb.

'Don't stop!' she said.

He glided his fingers further up her neck and further down her back. She tilted her head to one side and held her hair out of the way with her hand. Metal loops rattled down her arm and exposed her wrist and a delicate pattern tattooed into it. He looked closer and saw that the pattern was actually intricate script. He tried to read it in the flickering light of the television.

Let . . . the . . .

Her head tilted the other way and he rubbed the muscles there. The tendons in her neck shifted like webs of buried wire.

Let the . . . good times roll.

He stifled a chuckle.

She swapped arms and on her other wrist he saw another tattoo beside a white ridge of scar tissue. The hair on his neck stood up and his smile faded. He tried to read the tattoo.

Too fast to live, too young to die, it said.

Oh shit, he thought.

Tears formed and he wondered why and who they were for. Jade turned and saw them and Daniel tried to cloak his face in a smile but she reached up with both arms, wrapped them around behind his head, pulled his mouth down to hers, and kissed him hard on the mouth. He pulled away but she held his bottom lip between her teeth, looked into his eyes, and squeezed until more tears seeped from him.

He tried to say something but the sound that came out sounded like something dying so he stopped and as soon as he did she let go and stared at him and he stared back for what seemed like a long time.

'It was an accident when I was a kid,' she said and then she extended her bare legs, stood, and sauntered from the room.

Daniel sat for a while and watched the television but didn't see it.

Shit, he thought. His lip tingled and flashed.

Cliff wandered back into the room. He sat down in the chair and looked at Daniel.

'Where's Jade?'

'Gone to bed.'

His lip flapped in the breeze and felt as big as a house.

After a minute, Cliff said goodnight and left and Daniel sat with his head in hands and stared at the television until midnight.

Cliff slept soundly and had the dream again, except this time he was metal and nine feet tall and his head scraped against the ceiling. There was a fire inside him which heated the rusted metal of his skin to a dull red. Old pitted chrome on his face in a mirror. He grinned and licked his lips with a tongue that rattled like a chain. His arms were gun-blue metal and welded to his shoulders, his backbone the axle from a car; machined and gleaming. His ribs were filled with the guts of electric motors; windings glinted copper in the dim light. Jade was there and watched him as he stood on the step and reached into the sky, electricity arcing between him and the ground, melting his insides and dripping red metal onto the ground.

During the night rain fell but no one noticed and a flaming engine barrelled along through the bush.

Swimming in silk

Michael woke before dawn. He sensed company. The police sergeant reached over his body and entwined his hair in a gloved hand and extracted him from where he lay.

'Any needles, mate?'

'No.'

The sergeant twisted Michael's arm behind his back and held his other arm tightly against his side. When they reached the top Michael overbalanced and the sergeant let him go and he fell onto the side of the road and grazed his hand and arm against the gravel. He watched the cop's black boots.

'Are you all right, mate?'

'Yes, officer.'

'Are you drunk?'

'No.'

'Are you sick?'

The sergeant pressed the back of his hand against Michael's forehead and Michael reeled at the ferocious heat of the touch.

'No, I'm not sick,' he gasped.

'Well, hop up then.'

Michael stepped up into the paddy wagon. There was a derelict asleep on the seat opposite. They drove for a time and then stopped. The derelict yawned and Michael saw straight through his head to the steel mesh covering the window. The derelict closed his mouth and smiled at him. Michael shuddered and wrapped his blanket around his torn hand.

'Out,' said the sergeant as he opened the door.

He half fell from the truck.

'Off you go, mate. Find yourself somewhere to stay and stay put and no more sleeping under bridges.'

'Yes, officer.'

The sergeant drove off. Michael watched the truck disappear down the road. He looked at his surroundings and knew he was even closer to his destination. He walked to the side of the road and slipped between the trees that grew there.

Monday.

'I don't want to go to work today,' Cliff said. 'I want to stay here with you.'

'Well I won't be here. I'm going to work. I need the money.'

'What do you need money for?'

'Everything!'

'Okay. Don't get shitty.'

He rolled out of bed and into the bathroom. Jade could hear him singing.

She dressed impatiently. The room seemed too bright. The walls were coated with pictures of naked women. She sat on the bed and put on her shoes and glared at the pictures. She expected this kind of thing—had seen it before. She didn't think Daniel would have them on his wall.

She lay on the bed and lit a cigarette and thought of Daniel.

Thinking of Daniel made her angry and excited.

The pictures reminded her of Cliff.

She held herself up on one arm. She walked to the wall and stubbed her cigarette out on the glossy skin in front of her. She ripped the pictures down and screwed them up into a ball. She leant out the window, spun the wheel of her lighter and held the flame to the ball until the paper caught. She threw it and it fell in the grass and spluttered and hissed until the flames won out and the pictures dissolved into black ash and a cloud of blue smoke that hung in the air until the sea breeze caught and washed it away.

Daniel waited until he heard Cliff finish in the shower and then, after a while, start his car and roar off. He thought he could hear Jade arguing with him.

The house wrapped quiet around him once they had left.

He felt better. He knew he had to leave and he worried about what might happen if he stayed. He went into the kitchen and Susan was standing near the stove in a gown and fluffy slippers, making tea on the old stove; its blue gas flame warm in the kitchen. She offered Daniel tea in a soft voice and seemed unsurprised to see him there. She gave him a cup and he sipped it and let the steam float over his face. They stood silently for a moment then Susan walked back to her room and closed the door.

He felt sorry for her. Cliff could be an absolute prick.

He made himself coffee, gulped it down and mixed it with the tea, and then slipped out of the house and up to the waterhole. He was going to enjoy his last day before he had to go back. If your heart is aching take an aspirin, his mother always said. Ha Ha. He slid into the water and floated. The water carried him gently and he listened to the sound of it running over rocks. His mind disengaged and spun like a wheel and he floated until his skin was swollen and puckered.

He pulled himself from the water and lay face down on the rock. Birds dashed through the air and small animals slipped through the undergrowth but Daniel took no notice and didn't raise his head. He lay on his side and the arm supporting his head became numb. The sky held clouds that threatened rain. He lay on his stomach again. The breeze flicked over his body and made him feel as solid as the rock beneath him. He hummed a tune into the rock and imagined the vibration spreading and building and slipping back into his body like . . . like what? he thought. Like nothing.

He felt his lip. Too soft—too fat—for a boy. Hair too long.

He stood and his arm tingled and his head was sleepy. He stretched out his arm and rubbed the muscles in it. He looked at his watch and was abruptly aware of the quiet and how different things looked when a cloud blocked the sun. He lay back down on the towel as the sun appeared from behind the cloud. He imagined he was lying on a white sandy beach that curved towards a rocky headland. Surf pounded and sent plumes of white spray into the air. Children squealed and ran.

Insects flew by and rang sweetly against the bell of the dream inside his head. He watched bees searching for blooms along the bank and a dragonfly sweeping dementedly up and down the creek. He moved closer to the bank and watched water ripple across polished stones. Nests of purple leaves in the shallows. He reached and trailed his hand in the water and swallowed its gentle, gentle touch.

Cliff walked into the garage and Davo saw him and his face began squirming. He was angry.

'What do you think you're doing?'

'Coming to work.'

'What time is it? Where have you been? Where were you on Saturday?'

Cliff looked at his watch.

'It's ten o'clock.'

'Yeah, it's fucking ten o'clock! You've had your chance buddy. You can't fuck me around any more. Your replacement started this morning! Do you understand?'

'Yeah.'

'I'll send your money on. Get any tools that are yours and piss off, okay?'

Cliff said nothing. He collected his tools, carefully wiping each with a rag before putting them into a plastic shopping bag. When he had finished he looked around at the garage walls and walked out.

The sky was blue. The sun was warm and there was a slight breeze laced with damp slipping down the street. He walked around the block, concentrating on his footsteps, breathing deeply, listening to the world shifting itself through space: the electric hum of bees in a tree, the branches so heavy with blossoms they looked about to break. The sun slid into the street, picking out bricks, fences, yards and flowerbeds in yellow detail. Money lives around here, Cliff thought. Old trees spread their green glossy leaves across the wide street and nearly met overhead. The blooms of a jacaranda softened the cold stone angles of the church on the corner.

He watched a clergyman, his body folded, working in the garden behind the steel and stone fence of the church's presbytery. Birds looped and slid through complex manoeuvres in the clear air above the town. A tall woman with short black hair walked along the street toward the clergyman and the presbytery. As she neared the garden she pulled back her shoulders, lifted up her chin, and changed the way her feet met the ground.

She walked past the clergyman that way, but he did not stop what he was doing or look up from underneath the wide brim of his hat, neither did he turn to watch her walk down the street as she passed him. The woman continued walking and Cliff saw her relax the muscles in her back until she was walking as she had been before.

He went and sat in the park near the river and watched the water. He needed to see Jade. He needed a drink. As he sucked on his cigarette and thought of her he noticed that his hand was shaking.

When Jade arrived at the shop Roy was sitting and sipping beer from a bottle under the counter.

He was glad to see her. He moved towards her as she walked in but she slipped past him and disappeared up the stairs. He held himself—stopped himself—and went and poured the beer into the sink and hid the empty bottle.

The night before had been worse than usual. He had seen his wife walk into the room. She had laughed at him. The bitch. He could smell her. Stepping from the bathroom, steam, her light step, wet hair across his face to wake him up. When they were young. Her playful touch, her strength which had wound itself around him and intoxicated him like nothing else ever had. The way they slept with the house open in summer, the clear night breeze drifting through their room. The stillness in the middle of the night sometimes broken by the breathless energy of her dreams. Driving her in his car. Showing her his country. Its colour. The colour of the first car he had ever owned, chrome gleaming where it was parked under the shade of the frangipani. They had wished, as all young people do, that they would never grow old.

The thoughts swirled around in his head. He wondered whether Jade would understand if he tried to explain.

Susan put her mug on the verandah floor and sat down on the broken armchair and put her feet up on the railing.

She wondered where Daniel was.

After sitting for a while she went for a walk around the house. She stepped into the gloom of the old shed. Here, one Sunday, her grandmother had found her and Michael. They had heard a noise. He had stood to listen and she had seen the dust on his shoulders and the sweat on his legs. Neither of them had heard her soft step or expected her to be standing there watching them, making no sound.

'You're supposed to be in church,' Susan had said to her. She smiled. She felt teenaged again and nervous.

She saw a horse, laden with dust, hanging high up on the wall. A wooden horse rescued from a carousel with golden ears and a white blaze on its forehead. Her horse. The one her grandfather had tied to the fig tree with rope so it swung, too high and slightly dangerously. She had spent hours on it. She thought someone had used it for firewood years ago. Her hand winged around her face and stopped on her forehead, shading her eyes as if the horse were too bright and she turned and walked back into the garden.

She could see the bright bow of the ocean in the distance, blue and sparkling. She sat on the verandah. It was hot and she felt sweat pricking under her arms. She watched and the minutes stretched into an hour. The sky was a bank of blue and white that strained your eyes to look at. She stared into the nothingness of the sky until her eyes played tricks and she could see things tumbling and floating like pinwheels, whirling in the black part of her eye. She stared at the curved stretch of ocean and didn't blink until her eye was awash with tears and everything was blurred and underwatery. She felt irritable and ready to scream. The edges of memories were coming to life in the present.

She went inside and found the driftwood box.

She carried it up the hill and along the track to the creek. She walked quickly and soon her legs began to burn. She came to a log lying alongside the track. She remembered playing on logs as a child with Cliff, daring each other to hop along, to walk backwards. It was slippery and dark. She stretched out her leg and stepped onto it. She felt her weight and the texture of the bark through her shoe. Before, she had been as light as a fairy, jumping and skipping fearlessly. She stepped tentatively along the log with shaking legs and then jumped off when she reached the end. She laughed and listened to herself laughing.

The trail veered toward the waterhole. She looked through the trees and saw Daniel lying naked on the rock. He looked as though he were the slippery white core of someone taller and darker. His penis hid in a nest of black hair. He shifted around on the rock and scratched himself. She smiled, intrigued. Long hair hung untidily across his brow.

He had something around his neck. Flowers across his chest like a bandolier of soft bullets. She was surprised to see it, and a little impressed by his ingenuity. The flowers were faded purple and had yellow and indigo eyes in their centre which followed her and planted themselves in her eye as she watched. She almost went down; just to see him jump, but she thought better of it.

She squatted under a tree and scraped a hole in the earth at its base. When the hole was deep enough she put the box into it and covered it up. Finished with, she thought, unless something grows from them.

She remembered hearing at school long ago that if you swallowed seeds they grew inside you. Three of her friends had sworn and spat on their hands and hoped to die. So she had asked her stepfather and he had laughed at her and walked away and she had been so angry she had wanted to hurt him, tear into him with her fingernails and teeth. The same girls had told her you could catch pregnancy from a public toilet seat. Later, she had set them straight about that.

She remembered her grandfather pointing to the swollen veins in her grandmother's legs and saying she had been a bad girl and eaten seeds when she was younger, and that, sure enough, trees were growing, and those were the roots and one day they would turn her inside out.

She remembered and she was disappointed with the memory.

'What are they Nana?' she had asked.

'Nets to catch a tickle with.'

'How?'

'Like this!'

And she would giggle even if it didn't tickle.

She turned and walked back to the house. She wondered what to do and she paced distractedly along the hall and along the verandah. She tested the soil in the pot plants and discovered all of them were dry. They looked half-dead. She found the watering can and filled it at the sink and gave each plant a good soaking. She sat down and felt better for having done something.

The wind began to pick up and she felt the warmth of it like breath on her arms. Grit from the floor leapt into her eye and she stood rubbing it until tears came. Clouds came over quickly, birds skimmed through the air. Soon, rain appeared like magic from the blank sky; catching in the trees and gurgling down off the roof. Sky juice, her grandad had called it. She remembered him walking through the mud in his big grey slicker, into the long wet grass which would soak through your pants in no time flat. The cows watching her and Cliff with their big brown eyes, curling their pink tongues around sheaves of grass, and breaking it off with a twitch of their head. The stink of the yard, mud and shit. They would come back from the paddock and stand in front of Gran's old wood stove, wringing wet, steam wisping off them, hot cheeks and cold fingers.

She wondered if Daniel had seen the rain coming.

He hadn't. He heard the wind in the trees and then the rain and as he ran down the track the rain chased and soaked him.

Cliff went to the hotel and drank the rest of the day away. When it turned four he walked to the shop, his heart hitching as if connected to his feet with a bloody string. He stepped inside the shop but Jade was busy. He waited, slouched against the wall. Roy stared at him and he stared back.

A small boy, his face and hair brushed by a glimmer of light, green-eyed and open-mouthed, watched fish swimming in the tanks. Cliff saw him and couldn't see past him. He envied the boy's sweet freedom to be transfixed by something he had never seen before.

He remembered his grandfather taking him to buy goldfish. He must have been good. He was excited, he knew what gold was. He thought the gold would be in the head. It's what made them sink, their ballast, how they could swim. That made sense. He had taken them home and, left to himself, had caught them from their tank and, with a knife from the kitchen, had split them open like fruit and searched for the gold but found none. Then his grandmother had seen him and had come sailing out of the house with her eyes hot, face crinkled, and grabbed him by the arm, hard, and then—maybe she hadn't meant to—pulled him up by his collar and his feet had slipped and his face had spilt onto the concrete and smashed his nose and blood had spilt over the path and over the fish.

He hadn't remembered it for a long time: not since the last time Susan had visited.

It was nearly funny but laughing seemed like the strangest thing.

He leant towards the boy.

'There's no gold in goldfish, kid,' he said.

'I know that,' said the kid.

He waited outside, thinking about it. He wanted to tell Jade but she looked strained and tense. He wondered if she was as tired as he was.

He walked around the block, slowly, concentrating on walking in a straight line. When he came around to the shop again, Jade was waiting for him outside, smoking a cigarette.

'Where have you been?' she said and then made a noise deep in her throat and spat something into the gutter.

'Around.'

Doctors circle me like old bastard crows. I watch them now and then. They look at my old body with pity and prod it but I have forgotten it and I am smiling because standing behind them, leaning against the wall with his arms folded, a grin a mile wide, cocky as you please, is him, *watching them. Laughing. And with a nod and a wink to me he is off, work to do. A good joke! He walks out of this sick trap lean and solid, I can feel his footsteps shake the floor and hear his whistling.*

Later when I wake or sleep or open my eyes or close them, I can't remember which, there is nothing but the yellow light of the sun sleeping on the other side of the globe reflected and transformed into the cool grey shadows on the floor and there he is again, casting no shadow, startling me, standing very still outside the window wearing a hat, the outline of his face and open eyes as still as stone, but alive, watching me. The breeze touches him and sends his smell over me. But the smell is sick and sweet and I know it too well.

He's out there now again, but laughing and giggling, telling a girl a joke or two that are probably older than I am. It may be them who move things around when I'm asleep so I don't know if I'm coming or going.

Rain fell; sometimes steadily as if controlled by an engineer with his hand on a polished valve; sometimes wild, throwing broken loops of water through the air, onto the earth.

Susan listened and lay on her bed.

He came in as before; slowly, across the floor; draining colour from the room and out through his skin.

He picked up things from her dresser and juggled them, perfume, powder, compact and creams, faster and faster and higher and higher until they were hitting the ceiling, breaking open, and showering them with a sumptuous cloud. Not once did he miss a beat. His muscles worked under his skin and his skin cycled through the colours of the rainbow as fast as he could juggle.

'Shit, the mess!'

'You're going to have to clean that up yourself!'

She told him as much, in a voice that meant it, but he pinned her down, held her by the shoulders and would not move and as she was about to kick and scream he opened his mouth full of white teeth and started to eat the clothes from her body as if they had been woven from fairy floss and stitched with strings of toffee.

She laughed. It tickled.

He traced the veins blossoming on her thigh with his fingers, as if they were flowers trapped inside her flesh. She looked at his skin closely. Right down deep, even in the dull light, rainbow colours sparkled back.

He reached behind her ear and and made a sound with his mouth and she watched with unsurprised eyes as he pulled a peach from the thin air there, held it for a moment in front of her just long enough for her to recognise its shape, texture, colour, and then popped it into her mouth. It was perfectly ripe, flavour rippled and tingled across her tongue. She took a bite then he whipped the remains away and flung them out the window onto the green grass. He stretched out his bare arm again and pulled a pomegranate from the same loaded pocket of air and cracked it like an egg under her nose and offered the tiny red seeds to her on the tip of his finger and flung the rest away with his free hand as before. He produced a mango, a pear, an apple, grapes, cherries; made a different note for each one and each note seemed right for each fruit and that was just as it should be.

He plucked a whole watermelon from the air and threw it

one-handed onto the grass where it burst and sparrows and crows flew down and pecked inside its open red mouth.

He sang some more and cheesecake and chocolate and ice-cream appeared and he watched her eat.

She wanted him to stop, to stop surprising her; so he did. He lay down next to her and she watched him, touched parts of his body, wrapped her fingers in his hair.

She opened her eyes and watched a curlicue of dust spiral down through the air. She could hear Daniel's footsteps. She wanted to talk to him.

She closed her eyes. The man was sitting on the end of the bed. He began to speak but she couldn't understand what he was saying, as if his voice was taking a long time to reach her. She held up her hands for him to stop but he just smiled at her. His voice slid deeper and lower until she couldn't hear anything at all and the room hummed and vibrated and then his words decanted from the air into her body and tingled and burned like an itch.

She could feel his warm breath on her ear, whispering things to her that sounded idiotic and she bent her neck towards him to hear but he circled her ear with his tongue, digging into its creases and sucking on her lobe like a sweet. As he sucked, the itch she had felt before turned into a delicate burning rush that grew and grew until it took her breath away.

She curled her body and lay beside him like a cat. She listened to his breathing.

He was beautiful and she was sick to death of him.

Daniel packed his suitcase. Shirts, jeans, pants, underpants, socks, comb, razors. He threw them all in and sat on the lid.

He sat on the lid listening to the rain. He heard music but this time it was real. He could feel it through the boards.

He went into the lounge and Susan was sitting in front of the stereo in her bare feet sifting through a pile of albums. Daniel smiled at her and she smiled back.

'My grandfather loved music,' she shouted.

Daniel nodded and sat down on the sofa.

Daniel listened to the music. It was old-time stuff.

'Do you like it?'

'Nice,' he nodded.

She stood up and reached for his hands and he looked at her.

'Come on!'

He stood up. He remembered waiting outside a dance for his partner to arrive; crickets, wet grass, nerves and cigarettes. There she is. Disbelief until much later when dancing made even the girls sweat. Human again. As human as they would ever get.

They danced around. He felt awkward but she didn't seem to mind and soon he was feeling better than before. She found more records at the bottom of the box. Their dancing became more haphazard, wild impressions of dances they had seen in old movies. Susan was better than him; spinning around the room. The pictures on the walls watched them.

He could feel the sweat in the small of her back soaking through her dress. She felt beautiful. He wondered if she sensed his crude assay. He thought of her husband. He imagined them in a hot dark room, no sound except, maybe, music playing somewhere in the distance, then nothing except their own sounds. He was unmoved and he was pleased he was unmoved.

He stopped and sat panting on the couch and watched Susan continue.

She danced around him and twirled near him, too fast, and he saw a flash of black knickers and white skin. Embarrassed, she left the room, but reappeared seconds later as if nothing had happened.

'One more?' she said.

Daniel thought he could still see red in her cheeks. He couldn't remember the last time he had seen a woman blush.

He took her hand and they danced some more and smiled at each other and the smiles seemed to stand for a lot of things and each understood what they were. Neither heard Cliff and Jade drive up to the house, walk up the hall and into the room.

Daniel stopped dancing. Jade watched them blankly and then walked into the bedroom.

'Hi,' said Cliff.

'Hi.'

He followed Jade into the bedroom and closed the door.

'I got the sack today,' he said to her.

'What do you want me to do about it?'

'Don't know. Nothing.'

Cliff kneeled beside the bed and touched her body tentatively. He kissed her and she kissed him back and her lips and mouth were hot. Cliff slid his hand up her thigh until it brushed against her crotch but she pushed his hand away so he kissed her again and his hand went shooting up her leg again.

'No, fuck it, I don't want to!'

She hit at his hand and jumped over him and out the door, slammed it behind her, and ran out into the rain.

Cliff followed her but stopped in the kitchen where Susan and Daniel were sitting.

'What's the matter, Cliff?' said Susan.

'I don't know.'

'What did she say?'

'Nothing.'

'Why don't you leave her for a while? I'm sure she'll come back and you can talk about it.'

'But she'll get wet!' Cliff gestured with his hand.

'Well, she's a big girl. She knows to stand under something.'

Cliff looked at her disgustedly.

'Why don't you mind your own fucking business?' he said, but then, instead of walking out the back door, he went back into his room.

'God, what a pair!' said Susan.

'Mmmm,' said Daniel.

Roy stood at the top of the stairs in front of his door and turned and cast his eye over the town. Windows were squares of warm yellow light through the rain. He could see the shapes of people moving around in the glowing rooms, seeing to one another.

He went inside. Quiet. He turned on the light and the television and changed his damp and dirty shirt. Before he knew it he had an open beer in his hand. He settled onto the couch, slowly sipping the beer. He stayed there for hours until he began to hear voices behind him and he would turn but see no one. He slumped into the couch, not asleep and not awake.

He did not move from the couch except to get another beer. The gold on his finger snagged his sight and he closed his eyes to keep away that wild memory. He took a mouthful of grog and swallowed. He tried to drown her image and quiet the steel cables which floated in front of him and threatened to ground themselves at his feet.

It was Jade who reminded him of her. Jade moving a certain way. Jade, something precious. He remembered the day she was born and driving to the hospital from work, gripping the steering wheel until his knuckles were white and icy. Foot hard against the floor and he had not let up until he was in the hospital and then they had told him to wait. He couldn't believe there was nothing he could do, that he was worse than useless. It was like watching a mate cop it and being unable to do a thing. Then she had been there waving her hand around at him looking like she'd been out cutting cane all day. Red in the face. He could only look at them both and be twisted by things which he couldn't describe.

Jade's tiny pure body.

Now, after all this time, she was with him; but she was different now, changed. He sat up. His head throbbed.

He could smell the sea. He saw sandcastles he had built and his father sitting next to his car. A fire burning as the sun set and his mother chasing him and his brothers with jumpers to keep out the swift ocean winds. Burning steaks. He could smell the rich smell of onions and red meat mingling with the salt-laden air.

Then he was back in the flat.

The rain whipped against the walls and lightning illuminated the dark interior like the flash of a camera; freezing the shadow of his head against the wall. Blood was at high tide under his skin and behind his eyes. He ran his hands through his sparse hair as if trying to smooth the top of his scalp. He strained his ears for the sound of something which fluttered just behind his ear, tickling and teasing him. He turned, roaring; teeth ready to grind flesh and pop bones but there was nothing there. Nights like these he remembered Asia, the immense pounding of the monsoon, looking out across the roofs of the city and the spray and mist where the rain hit.

Somewhere in the long stitch of the night an intention tickled the inside of his skull.

Daniel walked to where Cliff was sitting in the dark on the verandah and sat down beside him. Neither of them spoke. Daniel fished in his pocket and found a cigarette packet with a single cigarette inside. He lit it and offered it to Cliff, who took a drag and handed it back, the burning tip rising and falling between them like a light on a ship at sea.

They sat looking at the valley until the cigarette burned down and then their eyes met briefly but even then they said nothing even though they both knew something needed to be said.

They sat.

'She's the one,' said Cliff, eventually.

'Are you sure?'

'Yep.'

Outside, rain sluiced off the water tank and ran down concrete supports wrapped in thick stockings of green moss and ferns.

Jade paced inside the shed. Water was spooling down from the corrugated roof in rows and digging holes in the bare earth near the door. In the dim light from the kitchen window she could see the inverted cones of ant-lion traps sprinkled across the floor. She sat down in the dirt and trickled earth into the traps with her finger. Every so often a drop of water would fall through the roof and turn a tiny dry section of floor into mud.

Daniel washed dishes as lightning flashed outside. Things seemed to move at the edge of the scrub, down between the trees and bushes. He imagined things watching him in there, black shapes hanging off branches, grinding their teeth, water dribbling across blank faces.

Jade sat until her legs were stiff and sore and her teeth were chattering, even though it was not that cold. She stood up and brushed the crumbs of dirt off her legs. She had pins and needles. She was disappointed that someone—*anyone*—had not come out to persuade her to go back in.

She slipped back into the house with her shoes in her hand and washed her face in the bathroom sink. She slipped something off her wrist and put it down on the kitchen table. She walked through to the lounge room. Cliff was watching television with Susan and Daniel but he did not look up as she came in even though the others did. Jade stood for a moment and pretended to watch the television and then, after a few minutes, opened the door to Cliff's room and went inside. Cliff watched her go in and after another ten minutes which stretched and stretched and stretched until he—and Susan and Daniel—could not stand it any longer he sprang to his feet, snapped off the television, followed her into the room, and closed the door after him. Daniel and Susan looked at each other. Susan shook her head. Although it was still early they drifted off to their rooms.

Cliff shut the door and stood behind it and Jade slid off the bed and reached and curled her arms around his neck and kissed him. She took off his glasses and put them down on the table next to the bed. She pulled at his clothes and then pushed down on his shoulders until he was on the bed.

He tried to follow her reckless body. He followed traces of old perfume and sweat. He stared at her sliding around under his raw, thick, fingers.

She watched him from behind her black locks.

Susan stood behind her bedroom door. She closed her eyes and pictured someone like Daniel and brushed the painted wood with her lips and felt her breath glide back to her. Her heart pounded deliciously. She realised that she could, if she wanted to, open the door and walk into his room. The thought froze her and the tingling in her body disappeared and was replaced by a solid trembling. She put her hand on the cool brass of the doorknob.

The house swallowed water.

A drip from the ceiling landed on her forehead and rolled down her cheek.

Roy walked down the steps and thrust a brass key into the wet lock on his garage. His hands were steady. His teeth chewed ghost meat.

He slipped behind the wheel of his big old Ford and turned the engine over. It caught first go and roared.

He drove carefully out onto the rain-slick streets. He was untroubled by the black seam of alcohol in his blood. It took him less than ten minutes to reach the house. He pulled over to the side of the road and left the engine running and the lights on. He approached the house from the rear.

He walked up the stairs, opened the door, his eyes adjusted to the light. No one in the kitchen so he walked across the kitchen, stepping softly. There were three doors in the hall and he stood in front of the closest and opened it. Slowly so they wouldn't even notice. There was a dark shape on the bed but he knew it wasn't Jade. He backed away and opened the next door and there they were on the bed like he knew they would be.

He slapped his hand against the wood of the door and it made a sound like a gunshot.

'Fucker!' he shouted. 'She's my daughter!'

The shout woke Daniel and he jumped out of bed. He listened and heard a thud and another shout. He stepped into the hall and saw Jade—naked and grim-faced—running at a man with her fists raised in front of her like a boxer. The man side-stepped her and grabbed a handful of her hair and pulled her past Cliff towards the front door. Cliff stepped after him but the man, without letting go of Jade, flashed the back of his hand out across Cliff's face and sent his glasses flying and his head smacking into the doorpost. Cliff slid to the floor, dazed, and blood began to spout from his nose.

'Who the fuck was that?' yelled Daniel.

Cliff found his glasses and slid them on.

'Her father!'

Before Daniel could say another word Cliff ran into the room and threw his clothes on. He ran out the door and his boots shook the house.

Roy sped home. He stopped the car outside the shop, gave Jade his jacket to cover herself, then pulled her close. His hand held her wrist tightly. He ran his free hand gently over her forehead, her cheeks, her neck. Veins in his hands throbbed like swollen rivers.

'You can let go now Dad,' she said.

Ah, there she is, hair like honey, eyes like an overheated sky. Waving her hand at me. Whatever she knows is buried deep. Her eyes wander across my bare body, colouring my cheeks, my neck. She knows more than her prayers, can you see, staring at me like she is, a tall brown bottle in the grass beside her and a cigarette between her fingers. Just standing there now, not saying anything, not smiling. She doesn't fool me. Her face is soft and young but her eyes are keeping more than one lifetime hidden and more than one death. Wrapped up in her young skin she has lived longer than I, been further, seen more. The years of her children's lives, the unborn and the aged, have been added to her own account. Eyes brimming with age, she is more than the sum of beautiful.

There is nothing else to say because all's been said, all's been done and no words can hold what did happen between us and what did not. She sits like a hot wire, like a thread in my mind and there's no operation to remove it that won't kill.

She smiles and her lips crease into a sneer, then a laugh. She swings forward and leans over me, grinds her finger into my chest. I breathe her in and shudder at her touch.

The last dream I had we were lovers in a room but then she waited at the window for another man to arrive and had no eyes for me.

But here's a young bloke I barely recognise. Grinning at me like an ape. He's down on the floor, messing about with something in the dark beside my bed. It's her, down on the floor, as naked as a baby, smiling up at me. Then he's on her, his strides around his knees. I can't speak, can't make a sound. I want to kill the mongrel. Skin the mongrel alive. They make a racket! The nurses will hear! They'll come! But no one comes and they go on all night.

'Strike me,' I say to them and they laugh.

The sun comes up. I watch the dawn and so do they. Then up come the strides and he comes over and winks at me and says, 'Big enough to fly the Jack on mate!' and laughs to bust a gut.

'Strike me,' I say to him.

Strike me.

Alexander Robert Whish thought his end had come when he saw her, once again, standing there, swimming in silk, staring at him. He puzzled over why she had come to him smiling like that, her eyes blue and wide, after what he had seen her do with the young man. He was too tired not to trust her.

She vanished from the room but he could feel she was still there. He could feel air moving across the bed where none had moved before. He sat up. He could move again.

'Well, I'll be,' he said.

He heard someone, or thought he heard someone, call to him. It was a familiar voice and he lifted his head to see if he could place the direction from which it came. He needed to see who it was. He gathered his strength but his heart coiled and sprang and he felt it stop like the click of an old joint and he saw, for a moment, not something he expected to see, but a little girl, just a bud of a thing, laughing and running across the grass, chasing something that flew through the air just out of her reach, and he needed to help her, needed to bend and lift her swinging up into the blue with strong brown arms but they were cold at his sides and he knew he could not help her and his heart fluttered and his last breath drifted into the night and did not return.

Cliff drove his car into town without catching sight of Roy's car and, perplexed, stopped in the lane behind the flat and sat and watched its dark windows. He lit a cigarette with shaking hands and wondered what to do. He wiped blood from his face with his shirt sleeve. The car filled with smoke and he opened the window to let it out. Rain fell on his arm and slid down onto the stained vinyl of the seat.

He could see through the window into the kitchen. The light was on. For a long time he saw no one. He had no idea what time it was. He pictured Roy standing over her bloody body; but then he saw him come into the room and sit down at the kitchen table among the dirty plates. Then Jade came in and stood behind him for a while, her mouth moving. Then she leaned over and kissed him on the cheek and walked out of the room and Cliff watched another light flick on and her shadow moving behind the curtains. Roy stayed at the table with his head in his hands.

The light in her room went out. He waited, he wanted to see her come out, see him, and run to him. Surely she would know he would be there.

From her room Jade saw him sitting in his car. She swore under her breath then went downstairs and let herself out through the front door of the shop and ran along the street holding a sheet of plastic over her head to keep off the rain.

Michael walked into Greenhill. He steered clear of the main street and its streetlights. He walked into a garden with the perfume of flowers and rain heavy in the air. He slipped through a window and stood in the darkened kitchen of a darkened house. Dishes in the sink. Containers neatly labelled. The refrigerator had a child's drawings pinned to it with magnets. He opened it and filled his pockets with a selection of items. He slipped through the window like quicksilver and followed the streets to another house. He stood outside it. He snipped off a dripping white flower with his overgrown thumbnail. He walked down the side of the house and tossed the flower between boards nailed unevenly across a shattered and blackened window.

He slept on wood and under a tin roof and hummed a tune he couldn't remember the words to.

'Do you think Jade's all right?'

'I don't know.'

'I hope Cliff doesn't do anything stupid!'

'Well, he's not drunk, so that's a start.'

'Do you think we should go and look for them?'

'Not in this weather. We could end up in worse trouble than them.'

'I suppose so.'

Susan sat down at the table. Daniel sat down with her. He had had to convince her that Jade's father was not coming back when she had emerged, pale and shaking, from her room.

'Grandad used to say Cliff couldn't see straight. He'd try and teach him things but he'd get so frustrated he'd grab his arm and shake him and if I said anything he'd look straight through me.'

'Do you think Jade wanted to end it with Cliff?' asked Daniel.

'I think she would have gone, sooner or later.'

'You think so?'

'I do.'

Cliff's watch was sitting on the kitchen table. Daniel picked it up. The hands were still. He shook it and tapped it against the table and it started ticking.

He wondered whether the roof would last the night. The rain was heavier than ever; pushed by an increasingly fierce wind. Water flowed in a stream down the wall in the lounge and out through a hole Cliff had drilled in the floor. Buckets and bowls were overflowing and the air was so damp his skin felt wet. One day, he thought, the whole joint will collapse into itself like a rotten tent.

'The roof sounds like it's going to blow off,' he said.

'I think it'll hold. I think the wind sounds worse than it actually is.'

'How can you tell?'

She shrugged.

The telephone rang. The sound broke through the wood of the doors and the rain on the roof.

'Shit, what's happened?' said Susan and rushed to answer it. Daniel waited in the kitchen. She came back and her face was pale as if she had left part of it behind her in the dark.

'My grandfather died a little while ago.'

Susan surprised herself by crying and not being able to stop. She was embarrassed when she realised that Daniel was still in the room with her. She felt light-headed.

Daniel didn't know what to say.

'Do you have to go down to the hospital?'

'No, tomorrow.'

'I'm sorry,' she managed to say to Daniel.

'It's okay.'

Her voice was ragged and edged with tears.

'I knew it would happen soon and I was ready . . . well . . . I thought I was ready . . . but maybe I wasn't.'

'Can I make you a cup of tea?' he said.

'Yes, that would be nice. Thanks.'

Susan went into the bathroom and washed her face and came back and Daniel was still sitting stiffly in his chair. A cup of tea was on the table.

She had an urge to telephone Thomas; to spoil his night. She wanted him to hurt the way she was hurting. He was also someone, she had to admit, who always knew the right things to say to her; the things she needed to hear.

She had a photograph of Thomas behind plastic in her purse. A picture of him standing at a mountain lookout. She had called to him and released the shutter when he had turned halfway towards her so his face was silhouetted against a background of hazy mountains and his eyes stared unguarded into the camera.

It was her favourite photo of him.

She held it as she rang. Their machine answered. She left a message anyway.

'It's Susan. My grandad's died. You don't need to do anything.'

Daniel stood in the hall, his arms crossed, his hands in his armpits as if something precious were about to pour from his fingertips and spread like a glaze across the floor.

She wanted to touch him; the slim packet of his hips.

He stepped towards her and took her by surprise. He hugged her and she took him in her arms and hugged back.

It was milk and honey. Cold water on a burn.

Awkwardly, they moved apart and Susan saw that Daniel's face was wet.

'I'm sorry about your grandad,' he said, and turned and left the room.

Daniel lay on his bed. He wiped his face on his shoulder. He didn't understand what had happened and didn't want to think about it. The wind howled over the tin roof and licked and bent against the sides of the house. He shivered. Gusts with extra muscle rattled the window and threatened to pluck out the glass like an eye from a socket.

Long white arms crept out from her room, under the door, up the hall and into his room. Bloodless fingers with dark mulberry nails.

He tried to sleep but couldn't. He felt her steps in the hall fading towards the kitchen. He opened the door a crack and waited, straining his ears. He heard the toilet flush and then he closed the door as Susan walked past and back into her room.

Cliff waited and grey curling sticks of ash fell onto his jacket.

When Jade didn't appear he ran out into the rain and up the back stairs of the shop and pounded on the door.

There was no answer and no movement inside the flat so he knocked again and yelled out.

'Jade!'

Roy came to the door and opened it. His face was red. He looked old and tired.

'Where is she?'

'She's gone.'

'Where?'

'I don't know. Try the hotel.'

Cliff, disgusted, turned and ran to the car.

He pulled up in the street beside the river and ducked into the hotel beside it. The front bar was crowded and he pushed through drinkers and searched the crowd for her. He couldn't imagine why she had come here.

And then he saw her.

She was with the same guys; the one he had hit was there: Russell. He walked straight up to her with the question on his face; grabbed her arm but she pulled it back and the men around her pushed him away and she turned away from him. Russell stood up but Jade shouted something to him and he sat down.

Stunned, Cliff stood amidst the drinkers. People looked at him. Some laughed.

He felt a hand on his shoulder and it startled him. He turned and saw it was Sim, the pusher.

'Sit down mate, I'll get you a drink.'

Sim steered him to the other end of the bar and bought beers.

'Shit, man, what's the matter? You're being very uncool.'

Cliff stared at him.

'You fell for her, hey? Well don't worry, so has half the town they reckon! Get over it, mate. She's not worth it.'

Cliff drank his beer but didn't taste it. He didn't answer Sim but looked sideways along the bar.

'Do you need anything, mate?' said Sim. 'Speed, trips etcetera. I've got some good trips I'll give you if I can tax some of your plants later on.'

'Yeah, okay.'

'Good on you, mate. How many do you want?'

'How many you got?'

'I've only got three on me.'

'They'll do.'

'Come on then.'

They walked to the toilets and Sim handed over the trips and Cliff put them straight under his tongue.

'Shit mate, that's too many! These are strong!'

Cliff said nothing and walked back to the bar and ordered whisky and drank it. The shelf behind the bar had a bottle sitting on it with some kind of deep-sea creature preserved in rum-coloured fluid. Pickled fish, a sign said on the bottle.

Sim came and sat next to him and watched him dispassionately. Half an hour passed. Cliff stared at the group in the corner. He watched Jade drink, laugh, smoke a cigarette. He almost smiled with her. She avoided his eyes and he saw that she avoided his eyes. He watched Russell and his mates, grinning, leering, smirking.

The juice hit. He felt sick and the floor began to roll. The fish in a bottle began to spin. He turned to Sim but he had disappeared and in his place was a man with a tattooed face and matching shirt. His eyes were light blue and floated gently in his lined and green face. Black tears glistened under each eye. Cliff looked at him, unsure of his vision, distracted by the light caught in the glass in front of his eyes. The man looked back at him. His eyes were glowing. Cliff stared. The man stepped toward him.

'You all right, mate?'

'Yeah.'

Cliff reeled off the seat and stood for a moment.

'You fuck, you stupid stupid fuck. Don't you get it? I was saying goodbye before!'

Jade was in front of him, talking to him. He heard what she said but it was meaningless. He thought her cheeks were wet, but then, everything looked wet, felt wet. He stepped away from her and collided with a circle of drinkers. One of the circle collided with more people behind them. They shouted at Cliff. He couldn't hear what they were saying. He could feel the cold wetness of the beer on his shirt. He still held a glass of his own, nearly full. He turned to walk away. Arms grabbed him and pushed him towards the door. He bumped into people, stepped on a woman's foot. Arms began to swing. He shot through the door. People followed him into the street. He walked away. He turned and looked behind him. More people were on the street. They weren't watching him but were staring at a pair of men who seemed to be biting each other's throat.

He watched a glass float through the air; tumbling end over end until it dissolved into the road. Then another. Then another in his direction. He watched it come, high and fast, catching the light from the streetlight. It smashed into the road near him. He watched the pieces melt and disappear. They took his breath away.

He looked around for his car.

He found it and found his keys and started it. He shifted into first and planted his foot.

Cliff drove down the road and the bones in his head hummed and he rubbed his tongue across his teeth but could not feel them.

The car grew longer, wider. The corners of the bonnet curled up and out in a screech of straining metal. Chrome on the bonnet grew in his eye. A tiny chrome girl lying back on the heat of the engine and then a tiny chrome boy on top of her with his head up and eyeing Cliff and licking his lips and Cliff stared back and his breath rolled around solid in his mouth and the wheel moved under his hands.

Freaky, he thought.

He dragged his eyes away to the road but the grass was moving and coated with light like sparks from a train so he watched the chrome grow again and become the lovers, growing and growing and then they were screwing on the bonnet and the car was bouncing on its springs and he could not see the road for their silver bodies filling the windscreen and then the girl's head rolled back and looked him in the eye and winked at him.

Cliff ducked his head, pressed his face into the red vinyl seat and closed his eyes hard. The car, still in first gear, rolled off the road and stalled when it bumped gently against a fence.

Through the hotel window Jade had watched Cliff find his car and drive away. She turned away from the window and slipped through the hotel doors. She heard someone calling her name but didn't look back. She ran along the road and across the bridge; caught the wet swirl of river smell in her nostrils. When she reached the awning of the shop she was drenched and out of breath. A sickle of wet hair slipped down off her forehead and across her face and she popped it into her mouth and sucked it dry.

In the blackest reach of night Cliff, glass-eyed and aimless, slipped from the swinging metal of the car and crawled away. With much effort, he pulled himself upright; his legs no longer his own. He could not see the lighthouse or the fig but he wasn't looking for them any more. He walked through nothing but rain and steaming mist. The ground disappeared from where it had been beneath his feet and he fell and kept on falling and could do nothing to stop himself. When he was still again he did not try to move. He could hear rushing water. Before he closed his eyes a gleam of gold as sharp as a knife streamed toward him and warmed his bloody face.

Something dripping with bells, rumbling with power, came to a halt in a blast of scorched air. He heard a changing tune which, as he listened, sang him to sleep.

THREE

Rain and smoke

The morning was as grey and dull as the night had been black. Swallows wheeled in the dry air above Michael and sat flicking water off their feather-coated backs.

He woke to the sound of the rain falling on the concrete bridge above his head. Rills of water ran off the metal railings and into the weeds. He edged out with his blanket still wrapped around him, held his head under the water, and washed his face with his better hand.

He went looking for a tap to drink from because the water off the bridge smelt of oil. He walked beside the river and into the park. He slouched over to the only statue in town: not an angel, saint, king or queen. He looked up at the soldier and saluted.

He found a tap and drank from it and then sat inside a picnic shelter scratching his beard and yawning. He saw a body at the bottom of the slope and waited a moment for it to disappear or move but it didn't so he walked over with his blanket over his head and squatted next to it. He touched the body's neck and found a heartbeat. He rolled the body onto its back and recognised him as soon as he saw the face.

'Cliff, mate!'

Cliff's face was white and Michael saw that his arm was loose and broken at his side and blood from a wound he couldn't see had stained the front of his shirt crimson. He

looked around but could see no one to help him. He pulled
Cliff up at the waist and then tried to lift him onto his
shoulder but he was too heavy and Michael swore and had
to sit and cough before he could try again.

Cliff muttered something and Michael bent over him and
tried to understand the words but they were soft and drifting
into each other.

'You'll be right, mate. Hang on.'

He tried again and managed to lift him upright and bend
his back across his shoulder. He staggered across the park to
the road, his trunk aching and his thighs already beginning
to tremble and burn. He reached the road but the cars he had
seen passing earlier had vanished and the street was deserted.
He crossed the road and struggled along the street that led to
the hospital. He waited for a car to stop beside him and offer
him help but none came past and he continued up the hill
with Cliff a fractured rider on his back and his body about to
burst.

Susan was almost ready to drive down to Greenhill when the
telephone rang.

After she had finished speaking to the caller she pounded
on the bathroom door and yelled at Daniel.

'Cliff's had an accident!'

'What?'

'Cliff has had an accident!'

'Hang on, I can't hear you!'

Daniel jumped out of the shower, wrapped a towel around
his middle and opened the door.

'Cliff has had an accident.'

'What happened to him?'

'They think he must have fallen. He's got a broken arm
and he lost a lot of blood but they think he'll be okay.'

'Shit.'

'Come on, get ready and come down with me.'

Daniel dressed and they drove to the hospital.

When they found his bed he seemed asleep. His head was deep in a pillow and his arm was encased in fresh white plaster. One of his eyes was only half-closed.

The doctor walked into the ward.

'We are concerned that he hasn't regained consciousness,' the doctor said. 'Do you know if he's on any medication or if he's used any non-prescription drugs recently?'

'I don't know; possibly.'

'Well, we have to do a few tests and then we'll know more.'

'Do you know when it happened or who brought him in?'

'He was brought in early this morning by a man but he had left before I arrived. Maybe you should go and speak to the police.'

'Do they know about this?'

'They found his car not long after he was brought in. They checked here because they found blood on the car seat.'

'Oh God, what a mess!' Susan sat in the chair next to the bed and rubbed her eyes.

'Try not to worry, his vital signs are quite strong. We'll keep a close watch on him and I expect him to regain consciousness fairly soon.'

'Thank you, doctor.'

The doctor walked off.

'What do you think happened?'

'No idea,' said Daniel. 'Maybe Jade will know.'

'Jade. Yes. I wonder what she'll have to say for herself. Look, I have to go and see the undertakers in about ten minutes. Can you stay here until I get back?'

'I was going to see if I could find Jade.'

'Oh, okay, will you come back here afterwards? I shouldn't be long.'

'Of course,' Daniel said. 'Do you think he'll be okay?'

'Yes, Daniel, I think he will, despite everything.'

Main Street was quiet. Susan parked the car directly outside the undertakers and went inside.

Daniel jogged across the road and sheltered under the shop awnings. He wanted to be somewhere else but his curiosity was leading him along the wet street. Most of the shops were in the process of opening and the pet shop was no exception. Daniel stopped just along from it and tried to see in through the glass. As he craned his neck, Jade appeared in the window and they saw each other at the same time. Daniel indicated to her to come out and she did so with a smile of pleasure.

'Hello,' she said.

'Hi. Do you know about Cliff?'

'What about him?'

'He's in the hospital. He broke his arm and nearly bled to death.'

'Really? Is he all right?' Daniel thought she didn't seem very surprised.

'They think he will be. Do you know what happened?'

'No, he was all right the last time I saw him.'

'Where was that?'

'At the pub.'

'When?'

'About eleven or twelve. Look, I don't know what happened to him!'

'Was he drunk?'

'I suppose he was.'

Daniel leant against a post and sighed.

'I don't suppose it matters much anyway. Their grandfather died last night as well.'

'Poor Cliff!'

'Yeah. Well, the old bloke was getting on. He had a tumour.'

Jade laughed.

'Sorry,' she said, 'I thought you said he had a tuna.'

Daniel did not reply. 'Look,' he said, 'when Cliff wakes up will you go and see him?'

'No, I don't think I will.'

'Why not?'

'I'm not seeing him any more. I told him that. It's not my fault if he did something stupid to himself.'

'I didn't say it was.'

They said nothing and then Daniel leant closer to Jade.

'What happened with your father?'

'Oh, nothing much. I handled it.'

'Oh . . . good.'

Daniel looked across the street. Children were running along the footpath laughing and getting wet.

'Remember when you kissed me?'

'Yes,' said Jade and smiled.

Daniel could see the anticipation in her face, her body.

'Doesn't matter,' he said, and ducked back into the rain to cross the street.

He pushed open the frosted glass doors of the undertakers. Smith and Sons, said the sign. There was nobody about. The cool green interior was like the sober elder brother of the hotel across the street. In the quiet, the smell of flowers mixed in with the faint smell of wax and disinfectant. He couldn't see Susan so he slipped back outside and waited. He watched as the sun emerged from behind thick cloud and sent steam wisping off the black bitumen, but then it disappeared and rain started to fall as heavily as before. His hair hung damp and matted against his neck.

He pressed his thumb into the polished brass plaque set into the wall and then stared at the blemish he had created in its golden field.

He went and sat in the car and fogged up the windows

with his breath and watched water slide down the glass. He
didn't know what to think. He knew that Cliff was quite
capable of getting *himself* into all sorts of trouble. He wanted
to keep his distance from everything.

Susan opened the door.

'Sorry I took so long.'

'It's okay. Did you get everything sorted out?'

'Yes. They're going to do it tomorrow. Luckily they're not
very busy. The notice will be in the paper tomorrow but they
said that everyone in town will know already. He said some
people might get their noses out of joint but I just want it
over with.'

'What about Cliff?'

'He wouldn't have come.'

'Are you sure?'

'Yes, I'm sure.'

They drove off.

'I talked to Jade,' he said.

'What did she say?'

'She said she doesn't know anything.'

'Do you believe her?'

'I don't think she's got any reason to lie.'

They drove up to the hospital.

'I'm sick of this bloody place,' said Susan.

They waited for Cliff to open his eyes but he didn't. Susan
walked up and down the corridors. Once, Daniel said something to her as she walked by but she was in another world
and did not hear him.

Jade took a break for lunch. She walked along the street
purposefully until she reached the barber shop and then
stepped through its doors.

The barber had the racing pages open in front of him, a
cigarette in his mouth, and was listening to a race on the radio.

He held a finger up to Jade like a conductor and listened to the end of the race and brought his finger down with a flourish and swore at the jockey and the jockey's mother. Jade sat down in the chair in front of the mirror.

'Cut it like a boy,' she said to him when he stood behind her.

'Why do you want your hair cut like a boy?'

'Are you going to do it or not?'

The barber shook his head at her. He looked at her hair and shrugged and started snipping. He cut her hair quickly, but he would stop now and then and walk over to the window and watch women walk by on the street outside. Jade watched her hair disappear and before she knew it she was outside. Her ears felt huge and red. She looked at her reflection in a shop window. The barber had combed it so she really did look like a boy, but a weird, country kind of boy. She ran her hand through it and tried to push it where it felt right but it didn't feel right anywhere. There wasn't enough of it. She expected people to stare at her but no one did.

She stopped at the milk bar and bought a bottle of water and sat on a seat on the footpath and drank it and lit a cigarette and smoked it. When she had finished she walked back to the shop and did a twirl in front of her father.

'What do you think?' she asked, but she was gone before he could answer.

His aching eyes watched her feet run up the stairs.

'You look like an angel, sweetheart,' he said.

Susan and Daniel sat and waited until night fell but Cliff made no improvement. Occasionally his arms or legs would quiver uncontrollably for a few moments and then stop. The doctor sent them home and promised to ring if there was any change. They drove in silence until they had nearly reached the house.

'Sorry about this,' said Susan.

'What?'

'Everything. I know you were planning on leaving today.'

'Don't be silly. I want to stay until Cliff gets better, if you don't mind.'

'Of course not.'

Susan turned the car into the driveway and its headlights lit up an expensive car parked at the side of the house. Susan saw it and Daniel saw it and he looked at her and knew that she knew who drove it.

'That's Thomas's car,' she said.

They ran through the rain into the house. Thomas was sitting at the kitchen table rubbing Curly's belly. He filled the room with expensive clothes and a heady fragrance. His hair was cropped close to his skull and his glasses were small and framed with metal. His eyes ran over them coolly, slightly amused. He was a head taller than Daniel and Daniel was immediately intimidated.

'Hello,' Thomas said.

'Hi, I'm Daniel.' Daniel held out his hand and Thomas took it and shook it firmly.

Daniel looked at Susan. She had a blank expression on her face and had made no move to greet him. Thomas stood up, kissed her on the cheek, and then put his hands on her shoulders and whispered, 'I'm sorry' into her ear.

'You didn't have to come,' she said.

Daniel stood awkwardly and waited for them to part. His teeth were chattering and he felt weary and ready for sleep. He excused himself and went into his room and lay on the bed and stared at the ceiling. He tried again to plan his immediate future but not only were pieces of the puzzle missing but the pieces he had were sick and distorted. He gave up. He heard the deep murmur of Thomas's voice during lulls in the rain.

He was startled when he heard Susan call his name and he held his breath until she called again and then poked his head out the door.

'What?' he said.

'Come and have some tea.'

He thought she meant food. He went into the kitchen. Susan had made a pot of tea. Daniel sat at the table and he and Thomas stared into their empty cups until Susan poured. Susan sat and drank, bending her head over the cup and breathing in the steam. Daniel felt uncomfortable. He felt like a chaperone. He wrapped his hand around the china cup and absorbed its warmth with his fingertips. He dipped sweet biscuits into the tea until they were a soggy mess. The gold on Thomas's finger caught his eye and held it.

Thomas asked Susan questions in a soft and even voice. Susan answered him in the same way over the rim of her cup. She told him what had happened to Cliff. She left out things that Daniel thought were important but he did not interrupt.

They spoke a language of familiarity; their lives caught up in a tightly woven braid that he could almost see draped between them. Susan sat with her legs folded in front of her and her arm slung across her knee. He watched her lips as she spoke. They moved much more slowly than most people's and everything she said sounded considered and reasonable. It slowed down his thoughts like an incantation and he found himself listening to the sound of her voice instead of what she was saying.

He was staring out the window thinking about Jade and Cliff when his stomach began to growl. He looked in the refrigerator for food and found some leftover spaghetti. He put the food on the stove to heat, but before it was ready Thomas had wandered off and then Susan did the same.

'Goodnight,' she said.

'Goodnight.'

He served himself a plate full of spaghetti. Curly came into the kitchen and his tail whipped against Daniel's legs.

'Poor bugger, you must be hungry.'

He found a tin of dog food, opened it, and upended it into his bowl. Curly tucked in. Daniel took his spaghetti into his room and ate it. The rain became heavier and he listened to the sound it made on the roof and was comforted by its dull clamour.

He fell asleep, but it only lasted a moment. A drop of water fell onto his face and he jumped up, turned on the light and saw the new leak forming over the bed. He pushed the mattress into the other corner of the room and went into the kitchen and found a spare dish to sit under the drip. He drifted off to sleep worrying about water, bare wires, electrocution.

He dreamed. Under a star-soaked sky he ran miles and miles along a dusty road. Behind him, on the horizon, over the ocean, a massive storm glittered and boiled.

'Watch out!' he heard people shout, 'this storm will wash away whole towns! People caught outside will be drowned where they stand!'

'I need you,' Thomas said. 'I don't think I can go on without you.'

'Don't give me that bullshit now.'

'It's true, whatever you think is going on is all in your mind. Why else would I drive all this way to see you? I wanted to be here with you.'

'I was managing quite well.'

'On the surface maybe. But the man was practically your father. It's like losing a parent, and now this thing with Cliff.'

'You don't even like Cliff, you never have.'

'I've never said that. I hardly know him. But his condition must add to your worry.'

'*You* add to my worry!'

'Well, I don't mean to do that. I am still your husband, aren't I? I just came to help in any way I could and to tell

you, when all this is over, that I think you should come back
and we'll work on our problems together.'

Susan was tired. She heard his words and wanted to believe
him, wanted it all to be over. They were seductive. She needed
someone, something.

He held her and nuzzled his head against her chest like a
small boy and she held his body with her arms and squeezed,
more for her own comfort than his. He hummed a tune
against her stomach. She breathed in his complicated smell.

'We'll see,' she said.

'Open the window,' he said later, 'the room needs cooling
down.'

'Are you crazy, it's freezing outside!'

'It's wet. It's not freezing. You must be cold blooded.'

'If you touch that window you can go and sleep in another
room.'

Thomas waited until she had gone to sleep and then crept
from the bed and lifted the window as slowly and as quietly
as he could and took a deep draught of air. Susan turned but
did not wake. The sheet fell from her shoulder and Thomas,
gently, put it back.

In the morning Daniel woke early and showered and dressed
in plenty of time for the funeral. He was uncomfortable and
felt like an intruder. As a boy, he had seen the old man sitting
out on the verandah but had never spoken to him. The fact
that Cliff was missing the funeral nagged him.

Daniel wandered around and waited for Susan and Thomas
to get ready. He walked into the kitchen where Thomas was
sitting and Thomas looked up but said nothing. Daniel sat
and watched him clean his cameras with a soft brush and

then load them with film. Susan took her own sweet time in front of the mirror.

Thomas finished with the cameras, glanced at Daniel as though he had forgotten his presence, then stood and walked to the bathroom door and tapped. Susan opened the door and they spoke for a moment. Thomas came back and picked up a camera and stood in front of the open bathroom door. Daniel was intrigued. He heard a faint click and whir, then Susan's voice as her breath sucked in, held for a second, then spat, 'Swine!', the word sharply edged and ringing clear through the house.

'Sorry, you looked quite beautiful,' Thomas protested, but she had slammed the door.

Thomas slung the camera over his shoulder and went and stood on the back step; just before the line of water falling from the roof. He watched the water fall and hit the step. He pointed his camera at it, adjusted something with his fingertip, and took a picture of that.

When Susan emerged from the bathroom she saw Daniel sitting dressed and clean.

'You don't have to come, Daniel,' she said, surprised.

'I'd like to,' he said, and she didn't argue.

Susan drove them into town in her car. Thomas sat in the front seat and Daniel sat behind Susan in the back. He felt like their overgrown and inarticulate son.

The church stood on a piece of land that bent into the river like a stage. In the open paddock next to the church cows stood with dripping hides and water spilling from their noses.

Daniel watched people and tried to look inconspicuous. There were a lot of old men with the inside dark of the wardrobe still clinging to their suits. Old ladies with antique skin; dresses like pressed flowers.

Thomas mingled among the people with his camera as if he was at some kind of strange wedding. Daniel shook his head. He saw Susan with her hands clasped by a pair of gloved hands. The elderly woman reached around Susan's waist and hugged her like a much younger woman might. Susan hugged her back.

Daniel couldn't watch. He stepped inside the church and sat down. The coffin sat gleaming under yellow lights. He was surprised at the number of people inside. He saw veterans with medals on their chests. Some mopped at their eyes. He wondered how many secrets lingered between them and would go unspoken to the grave. The clergyman began to speak and Daniel listened intently to everything he said. Then, six of the men with medals on their chest picked up the coffin and loaded it into the hearse.

After the service, people milled around and offered their sympathy to Susan, and Daniel, surprised, saw the old lady he had visited touch Susan's cheek with the back of her hand. Everyone seemed to know who Susan was. They knew she was married and some mistook Daniel for her husband and he pointed politely to Thomas.

He watched two women pacify themselves with cigarettes; the suction of their lungs carving deep cracks in their faces as they inhaled. He saw them eye Susan; look her over, up and down, and then whisper to each other.

Cliff opened his eyes and found his head buried in a soft pillow and pale walls like a sling across his vision. He could feel sweat breeding between his back and the sheets, down in the crack of his arse and creeping between his legs.

An old man without a shirt was standing by his bed. His torso was tanned and wrinkled. Skin the colour of old teak melted off his bones. His arms popped from his sleeves like two grizzled sticks. The skin on his face was blotched and cracked and there were areas of fresh pink like burn scars breaking out across his nose and arms as though something inside him was trying to get out. Cliff stared back at him in surprise.

'Hello, young fella,' the old man said good-naturedly.

'Hello. Who are you?'

He didn't answer. Instead, he began to recount sexual exploits. One of his eyes crackled with energy; the other was a blown fuse; a broken link to something he no longer needed. He related conquests of long-gone years in an avalanche of detail and Cliff had no choice but to listen.

'I was *born* fully armed, if you know what I mean,' the man cackled.

He was wavering in and out of focus. Cliff thought he could see a cigarette hovering at the edge of his mouth. Most of his teeth were missing and fine threads of saliva bridged the gap between his creased lips as he spoke.

He bent over the bed and whispered conspiratorially.

'They'll let you out young fella; don't worry about that. After you level out a bit. But not me. They won't let me out. Not until kangaroos stop hoppin'. I know too much!'

The old man laughed and slapped the bed and slapped his thighs. It sounded strange, rattling off the white walls, banging around the high ceilings.

The old man nodded and laughed again until they were both laughing together and had forgotten what was supposed to be funny.

'But if you want to get out now, I can show you how it's done.'

'How do I get out?'

The old man pointed to the window.

'Through there, my boy. Come on, follow me!'

Cliff followed the old man. He heard something fall and break behind him.

The old man walked to the window and stepped through it. Cliff followed and then hesitated in front of the glass. Through the window he saw an oily river, things blowing by on the breeze. He saw kangaroos dragging themselves across the grass with their elbows; their bones cracked and flattened inside them. Rain ran off powder-blue skin instead of fur. Their heads turned towards him and he saw their tongues flicking out of their mouths, eyes blinded by thick crusts of salt.

He grimaced.

'Can you stop this stuff?'

'Don't worry about it, mate. Come on, run at it!'

Cliff took some steps back and then closed his eyes and ran.

Instead of returning to the shop after her lunch break, Jade walked up to the house. She had her father's raincoat on but no hat, so by the time she reached the bridge her head was wet and water trickled down her neck. The river was brown and swollen.

She balanced outcomes and searched for instincts to guide her but found nothing where instinct should have been. When she thought of Cliff she became angry and she fed the anger until she had to burst into a run. She stopped running when she reached the hotel and paused for a moment under the eaves of its roof and caught her breath. Her chest heaved and ached. A couple stepped out of the hotel and stood with their arms around one another, oblivious to her. She watched them whisper and then smile at each other. She stared at them and the woman glanced in her direction and Jade turned away but she had already seen the woman smile and, just for a moment, include her in a world of certainty and order. Jade felt like slapping her.

When she reached the house she saw the strange car in the yard and wondered who owned it and what it was doing there. She walked up the stairs and into the hall and knew the house was empty without needing to call out. She hung the raincoat on a hook behind the front door, took off her wet shoes and wandered through the rooms. Dishes were piled unwashed in the kitchen. Lipstick on a teacup. The refrigerator clanked and droned. She turned and walked along the hall towards the front door and stopped and opened the door of Susan's room. Empty. Sheets were hung across the windows like sails. Dresses on hangers hung from the curtain rods and from old hooks and nails embedded in the walls. She saw a man's coat on the bed and bent and smelt it. She heard a sound behind her and jumped but it was only Curly. He sniffed her hand and wagged his tail and pattered back down the hall and curled up on the mat in front of the television.

The telephone rang and she ignored it and it stopped and then rang again and she ignored it again. She walked into Cliff's room and stood at the foot of the bed and looked around. The sheets were twisted and off colour. Tissues lay like snow on the floor. A jug of water from the refrigerator, warm now, its surface coated with dust, sat next to the bed. A sweet, stale smell. Water had pooled under the open window. She saw pieces of her jewellery on the floor and she bent and picked them up. She saw a sketchbook lying on the floor with a pencil holding a page open and she picked it up and opened it and looked at what was drawn there.

It was a girl. It was a girl who looked a lot like she did; floating on the page, just her body, with nothing else touching her, not a bed or the ground or a man or anything. Something like her own jewellery, but swollen into tortured shapes, covered the body. They were as if strange internal structures had been uncovered and coated with fine metal and slung along the body's length. It was nothing she recognised.

Jade closed the pad and threw it back onto the floor. She opened Cliff's wardrobe. There were only two things on hangers: a denim jacket and a black leather jacket. She saw the parcel at the bottom of the wardrobe and she picked it up, saw it was unopened, and opened it. She stared at the contents and ripped open another box. She ran her hand over a cold face, then threw it to the floor.

She went into Daniel's room and sat on his bed for a moment and then ran her hand along his pillow and picked up long dark strands of hair and looked at them. She reached for his towel which was hanging on the doorknob and wrapped it around her head. She looked at herself in the mirror propped against the wall and stared without expression at her own reflection. She considered the colour of her eyes, her bones under the skin, the red farm of pimples sprouting between her cheek and mouth. She tested her smile.

She lay her head on Daniel's pillow and thought of nothing. She heard a voice and wondered whether she had dreamt it.

'Missus! Missus!'

She ignored the voice and listened to her own breath but the call came again.

'Missus! Missus!'

She swore under her breath and then went to the door and said hello to the man standing there. He bent at the middle when he saw her and seemed to be bowing and she smiled to herself. He had two jars in each hand.

'Would you like some honey? I've got brushbox, beeauutiful! Ironbark. Clover.'

'I'd love some. How much?'

'How much do you think?'

'No idea.'

'How much have you got then?'

Jade reached into her pocket and found nothing but coins.

'Not enough,' she said.

'Oh well,' said the honeyseller, 'some other time.' He turned back toward the steps but then stopped.

'I'll do you a deal. I'll give you a jar if you'll show me what you've got under there.' He pointed.

'You want to see my *tits* for a jar of honey?'

'Yep.'

Jade lifted her T-shirt and watched the little man's eyes illuminate.

'Okay then,' she said, pulling down her shirt, 'give me my honey.'

'Which one would you like?'

'The sweetest.'

'Mmmmm. I should have known.'

He handed her a jar and then turned and was about to leave but instead he rested the box on his thigh and reached in and handed her another jar, and she took it and held it in her other hand.

He smiled at her and seemed about to say something but didn't.

'Thanks,' she said.

'The pleasure's mine, love,' sighed the honeyseller and, whistling, walked back down the driveway to his truck.

When Jade did not return from lunch, Roy locked the doors of his shop and put the red 'closed' sign against the window. He went upstairs, packed a small bag with shirts, underwear, an extra pair of pants, his passport, razor and soap.

He sat at the kitchen table and wrote his daughter a note in a firm hand. *Jade*, it said, *I have gone to find your mother and bring her back. I do not know how long this will take. Could you please* feed the fish. *I love you, Your Father.*

When the church service had finished Thomas, Susan and Daniel drove to the crematorium. It was warm in the car and Daniel's head was soon nodding onto his chest.

'I didn't realise he was so old,' said Thomas.

'My grandmother used to say that the men in our family held on to life until their knuckles were white and the women let go at the earliest opportunity. She said that was because the women were braver than the men.'

'Didn't he fight in the war?'

'Yes.'

'Well, that was pretty brave.'

'Yes, and stupid.'

'What happened to his medals?'

'He threw them away when he got back.'

They reached the crematorium and were soon watching the casket disappear behind a curtain. When the last of the mourners had drifted away Susan walked to the car and started the engine.

'Are you all right?' asked Thomas.

'I'm fine.'

'Do you want to go home yet?'

'I want to go to the hospital and see Cliff.'

'Okay.'

They drove in silence and Susan turned up a strange road. Thomas didn't notice but Daniel did and he didn't say anything. They drove past houses until the road became more potholed and then, eventually, turned into a dead end. Susan, with sharp frustrated movements, turned the car around and the wheels churned gravel off into the bush.

'Careful!' said Thomas.

They followed the road back towards the town and Susan slowed the car and pointed to a house.

'The town drunk lived there. He would drink at the hotel every night and walk home leaning against buildings and fences but he never fell over. When we were young we were afraid to say his name out loud. He said the rats in his house taught themselves to read from the westerns that were piled everywhere. He said they used to turn off his hot-water system to annoy him.'

Thomas laughed. Susan turned a corner.

'Who told you that?' asked Thomas.

'My grandfather of course.'

'Oh.'

'He told me the telephonist lived there and I pictured her stuck inside the house and never able to leave, never able to sleep, in case someone needed to call the police or the fire brigade. He told me a man lived there who could split a tree with one stoke of an axe. He told me a man lived there who walked from here to America and back, holding his breath across the bottom of the ocean and walking up onto the beach at Pilbeam with a hatful of shells. He told me he went walking one morning and sat down to rest on a hollow log. He looked in the end of it and there were three stars in there, only babies, shivering and twinkling, frightened, he said, because the sky was too big for them, too black and too cold. There was one at each end and one in the middle. He tried to coax them out but then the sun came up and when he looked in the log all that was left were three charred spots.'

'Do you think I was supposed to remember those stories?'

'I don't know,' said Thomas.

'Well, I remembered them because he stopped telling them. I was twelve, thirteen? He said I didn't need stories any more, that I'd changed.'

'He was from a different generation,' said Thomas.

'Yes, I know that,' Susan said after a pause, 'I'm just saying that I remember his stories more than I remember him. I never had the chance to talk to him about *real* things. At least you knew your grandfather. I never knew mine. I know hardly anything about his life, hardly anything at all.'

They drove on and Daniel crossed his arms and pinched himself to stay awake.

They parked in the hospital lot and walked inside and into the ward where Cliff was. His bed was empty and Susan panicked and shouted for a nurse. The doctor who had spoken to them earlier walked into the ward and saw them.

'We tried to contact you,' he said.

'What's happened?' Susan asked.

'Cliff regained consciousness. He's okay.'

'Where is he then?'

'Well, he regained consciousness and tried to jump out the window. He cut himself, not too badly. He's upstairs in our special ward. From the amount of drugs we found in his body we're fairly certain he's having a psychotic reaction to them. It's not uncommon. I've sedated him and he's comfortable but there's nothing we can do now except wait. Unfortunately, we have no way of knowing how long he will take to recover.'

They stood and looked at each other. Daniel expected Susan to say something but she didn't.

'Thank you, doctor,' said Thomas, finally.

They followed the doctor into the lift and were soon watching Cliff through a glass wall. The lights in the ward were dim; red and green lights flashed and glowed like eyes in the wall behind his bed.

'Come on, let's go home,' said Thomas and took Susan by the shoulder. 'You too,' he said to Daniel.

'Yeah, okay.'

Daniel leant his head against the glass and watched Cliff. 'Dumb mongrel,' he said. 'Dickhead.'

The doctor had gone and Daniel looked around and tried the door, expecting it to be locked but the door swung open when he pushed it. He walked over to Cliff and put his hand on his forehead and it was hot as if his brain were in turmoil and strung out somewhere in the soft reaches between sleep and insanity. He held his hand there until the uneasiness generated by the contact had left and then he took Cliff's hand in his and held it and felt its warmth and size and remembered his father's hand, his grandfather's hand.

Daniel thought he saw a tear or the ghost of a tear in Cliff's eye but when he looked again there was nothing. He rubbed his sleeve across his own face and sniffed and followed the others outside.

As soon as they stepped through the door Susan and Thomas went into Susan's room and closed the door after them. Daniel walked around the house emptying containers of water into the sink. He turned on the radio in the living room and listened to flood warnings and road closure announcements; the even tone of the speaker was reassuring and calm and he promised clearing skies. Daniel turned on the television and watched it for a while but nothing held his attention. He wasn't hungry. He drank one of Cliff's beers and toasted him in his absence.

When his eyelids began to droop he turned the television off and headed for his room. He opened the door and in the light from the lamp saw Jade lying asleep on his bed. Her shape itched into his eye, his tired head.

'Bloody hell,' he said. 'Goldilocks.'

He closed the door and turned on the light and she woke up, slowly; shielding her eyes.

'What are you doing here?' he asked.

'Sleeping.'

'I can see that. I don't think Susan would be too pleased to see you.'

'Don't be angry, Daniel. I didn't want to stay with my father. I don't trust him. I don't care what Susan thinks. I didn't do anything to Cliff.'

'He tried to jump out the window. The doctor said he had a psychotic reaction to drugs.'

'Is he all right?'

'Yeah, he's fine,' he said sarcastically.

'Well, don't look at me! I didn't make him take drugs!'

Daniel sat down on the bed.

'Shit, what a mess,' he said.

'It's not that bad. Cliff is going to be okay. What's the problem?'

'You! I don't want Susan to see you! She'll freak!'

'Really?'

'Yeah.'

'You like her, don't you?'

'She's in there with her husband,' he said, and jabbed with his thumb.

'Oh, I thought they were finished.'

'What do you mean?'

'They were having problems, that's why Susan came here; to get away from him.'

'Oh, right.'

They sat for a moment and Jade ran her hands through her hair and rubbed her eyes.

'What happened to your hair?'

'I had it cut. Do you like it?'

'It's nice.'

'What's Thomas like?'

'He's all right.'

Jade smiled at him and he shook his head at her and smiled back.

'So, can I stay?'

'There's nothing I can do to stop you. But you're sleeping in Cliff's bed.'

'Okay.'

Michael squatted under the square sheet of plastic he carried folded in the pocket of his filthy jeans. He held up his aching

arm and the rain softened the dried blood there and sent it
in fresh trails down inside his shirt. He watched the house.
He watched the lights behind the glass. Red and blue over
the doors, over the windows. He watched the shapes of
people move through rooms. Warmth. He scratched the skin
at his neck.

When all the lights had gone out he went down and circled
the house. He peered into the twin darknesses of the shed
and the garage. He ran his hand across the steel of each car
body. When he came to Thomas's car he noticed the rear
driver's side door was unlocked. He smiled to himself,
checked the house again, and then opened the door and lay
down across the back seat. He fell asleep with the new car
smell strange in his nostrils and rain drumming on the roof.

As he slept he stirred a crucible of molten metal with his
bare hands and the heat seized the flesh and burnt it away
and left the chalk white bones parched and slack and rattling
against each other.

Jade was pacing the length of Cliff's room smoking a cigarette
when the light from the lamp suddenly winked out. She
crossed the room and flicked the main light switch but nothing happened. There was no light seeping under the door. She
listened but heard no movement. She opened the door quietly,
stubbed out her cigarette on the floor, picked up the jars of
honey and stepped into the hallway. She tiptoed into the
kitchen and sat the honey on the table. She opened the utensil
drawer and felt for a knife, found one, considered each jar,
and then chose one, opened the lid and sniffed its contents.
She slid the knife into the thick honey and lifted it above her
head until a gossamer thread fell across her face, neck and
chin. She loaded honey into her mouth with the knife until it
overflowed, then swirled her tongue around, tilted her head
back and swallowed it whole like an oyster or an egg.

She knifed more honey into her mouth and then held the knife between her teeth. She picked up the jar and walked to Daniel's room, opened the door and slipped inside. She sat down next to him on the bed, held his shoulders down against the mattress as he went to sit up and kissed him on the mouth.

Daniel let her slip the load into his mouth. It was so sweet his teeth hurt. He pulled away, their lips still connected by strings of honey until the slender candy collapsed like a cut rope between them. Jade lapped at his mouth and watched his face and Daniel stared up at the dark shape of her.

'You know what honey is don't you, Jade?'

'What?'

'Bee vomit.'

'Aaaarrrrhhh!'

She bent, smiling, over him and reflexively pulled hair from her face and put it behind her ear even though there was no hair there any more. She didn't seem to notice that she had done so and Daniel smiled.

She kissed his mouth again and the heat of her tongue was intense and he was surprised to discover that he didn't really want her to stop. He didn't want to think about what it meant, or think about Cliff. Her hand rested on his neck and she hooked one finger under his necklace and rubbed the bones in his chest with the others. Past the honey she tasted of cigarettes. He chased the sour taste across her lip. There was more on her breath, down inside her. He opened his eyes and she pulled away.

'Don't look at me like that.'

'I can hardly see you!'

Jade didn't reply. Daniel wondered if either of them knew what they were doing and why they were doing it. He thought not.

'I don't want to have sex with you,' said Jade.

'Oh. Should I be offended?'

'No.'

'Well, good.'

'Can I stay with you tonight? I can't sleep in that room.'

'Do you promise not to try anything else?' Daniel was half-joking but Jade answered him seriously.

'I promise,' she said.

This place I've dreamt of all my life.

Two storeys, three; maybe more hidden inside like a magic trick. A blanket of leaves over the ground. Verandahs wheeling around the outside of each floor; thick wooden louvres hold light away from the centre of the house. The rooms shrouded, musty, dripping with spiders and drifts of dust. Spiral staircases disappear into blackness and the ground underneath like wells. Stand at the bottom and you could see the sky through the roof. Beams as thick as trees. No one here who should be. I walk around, breathe the rot, searching for something, throwing up the dust until I can't see my hands in front of me. The house shudders and shifts. I look out between rough wood and see nothing but trees, the river, a black black sky.

Some-other-where

Thomas moved over to Susan's side of the bed, held himself over her, kissed her gently. His breath tickled her cheek. His kisses seemed awkward until she responded and helped him. Lapping at each other's mouth. She pulled at the cropped hair at the nape of his neck and felt the smooth grain of his city boy skin. Their clothes vanished. She held him tightly.

'Do you want to do this?' He was incredulous.

'Yes,' she answered.

He pressed against her and his weight pushed her down on the bed and she winced at the pain still lurking in the healing skin between her shoulder blades.

'What?' he said.

'A box fell on my back.'

'Let me see.'

She turned onto her back and he touched her where the skin had been broken and pressed his lips gently against it and the sensation was like ice on her skin. She wondered if she would have a scar and whether the scar would ever again have the same sense of touch or whether it would be numb and cold forever.

Thomas lay beside her and stroked her back. The bed and the sound of the rain made him drift off for a moment but he woke as Susan stretched and sat across him. She took him by surprise. He surrendered his uncertainty to the rush of her mouth and skin. She's not herself, he thought, and realised that neither was he. He was some other man, some other where. He saw the novel, careless, angle of her head and knew he was super-fluous to its production. He stopped moving and his theory proved itself. He resented each sound that escaped between her bitten lips but knew he could not afford resentment. He held her waist and watched the faint silhouette of her head and shoulders against the grey square of the window.

He almost felt the density of the thing which shook and shook her body until she bent and rested against him.

'Come back with me,' he whispered to her.

She took some time to answer him. His tone was too ordinary.

'I have to stay with Cliff.'

'He'll be fine. He'll get better and do it all again next month.'

'You think so?'

'I do.'

'He's my brother.'

'No one would ever guess it.'

Susan looked at him and then reached for her underwear.

'Come back with me.'

'I'll have to think about it.'

'Well, I wish I had the luxury of time you seem to have. While you think, our business is going to shit.'

'It was going to shit before I left.'

'Thanks. Thanks very much!'

Thomas rose from the bed. He flicked the light switch and when nothing happened he swore, dropped to his knees, found his bag and proceeded to stuff his clothes into it.

'What are you doing?'

'Leaving.'

'Now?'

'Yes!'

'It's raining!'

'I know. I've got a job tomorrow. If I leave now I'll just make it.'

'Don't be stupid. Roads are flooded. You'll fall asleep!'

'I'll grab some coffee! Bye!'

He walked from the house and Susan heard the roar of the car engine and then just the rain again. She sat up on the bed, pulled her legs up and held them in her arms.

After her anger, in behind it, she found calm. She was grateful to him and she wondered whether it would ever be possible for him to understand what she was grateful for.

Her heart drummed a message against her ribs.

Michael woke as Thomas slammed the car door and started the engine. His chance to slip from the car was spoiled by the cloud of sleep across his eyes. He lay still and tried not to laugh. He looked at the driver. He was driving fast but the car clung to the road. Michael wondered what to do. He didn't want to startle him.

He sat up behind the driver's seat but Thomas was grinding his teeth and didn't see him. He looked out the window. He swallowed and leaned over between the seats.

'I need to get off,' he said, and showed his teeth.

'Shit,' said Thomas, 'who are you? What the fuck do you want?'

'I want to get out.'

'Bloody hell!'

Thomas jammed on the brakes and as he did so the road bent suddenly and he over-corrected the steering and the rear of the car lost grip and slid off the side of the road, slithered down a short slope and fell upside down into a swollen brown creek. Michael tumbled over in the back seat and saw the glass in front of his nose fill with brown and then the brown rush in.

He pulled down on the door lock and then pushed the door open with his legs and slipped out into the water. The car bumped along on its roof and Michael was pushed along beside it. He waited for the man to follow him and break the surface like a swimmer in surf but he didn't. His feet touched something solid and he found footing and stood. He watched the car and the water's speed. He coughed and shouted but the faint outline of the car slipped under the water and disappeared in a blink. He turned and ran away.

The water in the car was cold and then warm. It stripped Thomas's defences with a billion swirling drops until no defences were left and Thomas was separated from the world with a snap.

In the morning Daniel woke and saw Jade sitting straightbacked on the edge of the bed. She was silent and still and her thin back was damp with perspiration as if she had been struck fresh from a mould. Daniel, watching, became as tense as the muscles clenched along her spine. He wondered whether he would be intruding if he reached out and touched her.

Light streamed through the window and Daniel blinked at it in surprise. He saw blue. Jade turned and saw he was awake and pulled her shirt over her shoulders.

'The rain's stopped,' he said.

'I know.'

'It's a beautiful day.'

'Yep.'

'What's the matter?'

'Nothing.'

Jade stood and headed for the door and, before Daniel could say anything, opened it and headed for the bathroom. Daniel put on his shirt and pants and hovered around the doorway. Susan came out of her room and she was already dressed and he noticed that the creases in her forehead were gone. She smiled at him and he saw the pink rail of her gums.

'Good morning, Daniel.'

'Morning.'

She heard the shower running.

'Who's that in the shower?'

'Ah . . . Jade.'

'Oh.'

She walked into the kitchen, lit the stove, filled the kettle with water and left it to boil. There was nothing to say. To offer her an explanation would have been an admission that he owed her one. They had left too much unspoken. How could he explain something he didn't understand.

The kettle boiled and Susan made tea. She poured two cups and sat down at the table and sipped hers and Daniel sat and did the same.

He ran the fine china across his lip and tried to ignore the emptiness he felt.

Jade stepped from the bathroom wearing a dress covered in flowers. Her skin was pink and clean. At three paces, Daniel could smell the soap still on her. She stopped when she saw Susan.

'I don't want to be rude,' Susan said pleasantly, 'but I think it's time we were all moving on.'

Jade shrugged her shoulders.

'Sure,' she said, and reached and took a pinch worth of Daniel's shirt and pulled it gently.

Daniel packed his suitcase and Jade watched him.

'Bitch,' she said.

'She's not a bitch.'

When they emerged from the room Susan was nowhere to be seen and Daniel was disappointed. They walked out the door and Daniel put the suitcase in the car's boot and noticed Thomas's car had gone.

Black-bellied clouds swirled over the valley rim as Daniel slipped behind the wheel of the car and started the engine. He was about to turn his head to reverse when he saw Susan run down the side of the house and stop, breathless, beside the car.

'I didn't think you'd be so quick!'

Daniel climbed out and stood at the side of the car. The engine was still running.

Susan reached over to Daniel and kissed him goodbye and that was for herself more than anything. She kissed an idea of him that floated around his body like a dream; like an old friend. When they separated the lipstick she saw smeared across his face seemed appropriate.

The first kiss and the last, sunshine.

'Thanks for being so sweet,' she said.

'That's all right. I hope everything turns out okay.'

'It will.'

Susan could see Jade staring at her and she was amused by that. Daniel waved to her as the car accelerated away. When they had gone, Susan walked around to the rear of the house. Some of Cliff's clothes—which had been hanging on the clothesline since the rain started—swung wetly like newly flayed skin. Magpies raked over the wet grass and pulled out grubs and worms. Susan picked flowers she found hidden among weeds and thistles. Stunted red roses like the hearts of tiny animals. Lilies in the shelter of the house. Drops of water, like the sweetest of tears, hung from the belly of everything and sparkled in the sun. She closed her eyes and saw fountains and rainbows.

She moved out of the shade and the sun flashed on the silken metal that swam and looped over the bones at the base of her neck. A cloud slipped like a cushion under the sun. She walked inside the empty house and a cricket began to sing like a drill in the grass.

'Do you want me to drop you off somewhere?' Daniel asked Jade.

'Aren't you going to stay?'

'I have to go.'

'Where do you have to go?'

'I don't know yet.'

'Come to the beach with me.'

'I can't.'

'Please!'

He looked at her.

'Okay,' he said. 'Then I'm going.'

They drove through Greenhill. Jade saw the 'closed' sign in the window of her father's shop, wondered about it, but said nothing to Daniel. It was almost strange to see people out, the town breathing again after the rain. School. Shopping.

Daniel saw a girl waving her distorted arm at cars driving by. An older girl, fine limbed and tall, who might have been her sister, stood with her arm draped across the younger girl's shoulders. She held her chin high.

Daniel stared at them and the older girl saw him staring and raised her finger in his direction. Jade saw it and laughed at Daniel and laughed harder when she saw the red flush on his neck and cheeks.

'You should have waved back,' Jade shouted.

'You're hilarious.'

'I know!'

They drove past the hospital and Daniel slowed and studied the walls and the windows. He felt sick in the stomach.

'If you want to see him let me out and I'll go to the beach myself.'

'He's my friend.'

'He might be awake. He might see you driving me away.'

Daniel didn't stop.

'It doesn't matter what you say,' he said, 'I know you feel bad about it.'

'I don't.'

'Yes, you do.'

'Are we going to the beach or not?'

They drove and Jade hung her head from the window and let the wind blast through what was left of her hair. Daniel laughed at her even though he tried not to. The beach was nearly deserted. Jade sprang from her seat and had crossed the car park and was halfway down the sand before Daniel had locked the car. He followed her, left his clothes and shoes beside her dress, and walked down to the water's edge. He waded into the surf until he was behind her. Someone had once told him to look out for women who wore matching underwear. Jade wore black and it made her skin look even paler.

She splashed water over him and he splashed her back and in the midst of a foaming wave she launched herself at him and gave him the second best kiss he had ever had.

'What do I taste like now?' she asked him.

'Salt,' he told her, spluttering. 'Why do you keep kissing me?'

'I like kissing you! You're nice. You're sweet, like that bitch said.'

'She's not a bitch and I'm *not* very nice. I'm not a very good friend either.'

'Maybe I don't want to be friends with you,' she said, and then walked from the water.

Daniel followed her up the beach and they found a tree with shade and Daniel went to the car and found a blanket in the boot and he spread it out under the tree and they sat on it. Jade sent Daniel to the shop for food and they sat on the blanket and ate with their fingers.

'If you had money, where would you go?' Jade asked.

'I don't know. Nowhere. Where would you go?'

'I'd go to Paris and let a beautiful Frenchman kiss me. He would have to climb the Eiffel Tower to earn it. Or maybe I could just kiss you and close my eyes and pretend *you* were a beautiful Frenchman.'

'It wouldn't be the same.'

'Maybe it would be better.'

'I doubt it.'

'Do you?'

'Yep.'

He watched her walk down to the water again. She stopped and turned her head towards Daniel and shouted something. Her teeth flashed, her words span out into the air. She gestured with her hand for him to follow but he shook his head. He watched her swim. She dived into waves and went further and further out until her head was just a black spot. She could have been anyone.

She stayed there for a long time and then, slowly, made her way back.

When she reached him she shook the water from her hair and sent drops of water in an arc over him.

'Thanks,' he said. 'Put your dress back on or you'll burn.'

'Yes, Mum.'

She stoppered a nostril with her finger and blew water out of the other.

She held up her arm. Her veins stood out like a pattern of limbs in a tall tree. They ran up her arm in green and blue.

'Don't you wish you could change colour?'

Daniel looked at her, skin sure and untroubled.

'Maybe,' he said.

'Of course you do,' she said and ran across the golden afternoon sand and turned a cartwheel.

He ran after her. He wasn't sure why he did. He held the soft inside of her arm but she pushed his hand away, gently, and kept walking.

'I want to come with you,' she said, surprising him.

'I don't know where I'm going.' He held his hands up in front of him.

'We could go where I want,' she said.

Daniel stood for a moment and watched her walk away and felt something cold in his stomach that grew and grew as she moved further away. He didn't want to say goodbye again. Not yet. He caught up with her.

'We could go where you want,' he said.

The day faded and they walked along the beach until they came to the place where Cliff had started a fire. Daniel lay on the blanket and Jade hunted for dry sticks and lit a spluttering fire against the blackened log of driftwood. Clouds incandesced and the sky became more than sky. Jade lay in front of him with a shade of sunset on her forehead.

He pulled her close and looked at her. She tried to pull away but he held her.

'Let me look at you.'

She let him, but only for a minute.

He was so close to her that she wasn't beautiful, wasn't ugly, wasn't a person any more, wasn't even a face, just two eyes, a nose, red fissured lips, the scar on her cheek, and the teeth behind her lips white and hard until the red slipped over and softened them.

And then she was smiling at him, laughing again.

'What are you doing?' she asked.

He looked into the dark yolk of her eye.

'I don't know,' he said, and laughed.

He lay back on the blanket and watched her feed the fire and sit in its flickering orange light. He fell asleep with the base notes of the sea and the smoke all around him. When Jade saw he was asleep she curled up beside him and leant her head against his. She stayed awake long into the night, slipped into a shallow sleep after midnight, and woke again before dawn.

The sky dripped a pale slick of moonlight onto the sand.

Jade watched the day emerge from the blackness, whole and clean, swelling from purple to blue over the ocean. Daniel's head was still in the crook of her arm and her arm was numb from shoulder to wrist. His skin was soft. Whiskers on his chin the only thing betraying his sex. She touched his face and he was cold at the mouth.

Even after everything, even if it all disappeared in the daylight she would remember this. She held his head and cold cold fear poured through her, wrapped itself around the weakest, gentlest, part of her, and tightened. She fought it. She fought it with her teeth clenched and her hand wrapped in his hair and, slowly, her body, and the air around her body, was warmed by the ancient operation of morning and the air over the shore became an undreamt of ocean of clean hue and shade and she became a part of it and her skin began to glow until it was consumed by, and flush with, its own colour.

Michael could smell the smoke from their fire hanging over the beach. He saw the dark shape of them together and wondered dreamily who they were and what they were doing. He felt thin and faded and about to be spun off the earth into the black gap which floated just above him. He lay down at the edge of the sand. A lizard, disturbed by his feet, rustled through the bush.

'Sorry, mate,' he said.

He slept, or thought he did, until something made him look up. Someone was sitting across from him, wide-eyed, dark spaces where a body should have been. A woman, he thought, but wasn't sure.

'Are you an angel?' he said.

'No,' she laughed, 'I'm just your poor tired mind playing tricks on you!'

'Oh,' he said. 'Bugger.'

'Come on!' she said, and held out her arms to him.

He moved towards her, moved to touch her but her body was a black hole which swallowed him, consumed him up to the shoulders, and the dark spaces were not spaces at all but the coolest water. She smelt of smoke and spice and water and salt and sea breeze all together. The cool blueness spread from his fingertips into his hands and then rushed through every strand of him and spread into every crack and crevice and formed a seal and filled gaps in his memory he didn't know were there.

She pulled him to his feet and he ran along the sand behind her, bright with energy, along beneath the dark sky, and then they ran along the edge of the water and then into the water.

He plunged into the indigo swells and she followed him and clung to him like a shadow. Safe underneath until the burning pain in his chest unfurled and sent him back, rippling clean up through the blue. Then she was at his side again and they were up in the dunes and floating on the cool white sand and the sky was flush with stars and he was short of breath and a mosaic of salt was drying on his skin.

As quickly as she had come she had gone and he knew that he was absolutely alone and, in so knowing, remembered all the things he had forgotten.

Honey from the comb

Susan made herself breakfast and then closed up the house as best she could. She opened her camera and exposed the film to the light and threw it on the floor. She took the telephone off the hook and lured Curly into the car with biscuits and a sweet tone. She closed the front door and pushed the bronze man against the door to hold it shut. Unable to help herself, she rubbed his fat belly for luck and turned away.

She drove to Greenhill with Curly barking in her ear. The sun was already high in the sky. She stopped near the post office, found an address for a kennel in a telephone booth's torn directory. She drove to the kennel and booked Curly in indefinitely and paid with cash. She drove back to Greenhill and up to the hospital. She walked to Cliff's room and her breath was short when she reached him.

The room was still and heavy with humid air. Cliff's forehead was creased as if he slept a troubled sleep. His face looked younger without his glasses and there was a suggestion of beard on his chin. A fan sprayed air across the room. Chimes far away rang and tinkled.

She shifted and bent over him, held her breath, studied his face and neck and the hair wound around them. Pale skin, bright lips. Quite still and asleep. She leant down and felt the warm stream of his breath and saw her own nervous breath sweep across his face making stray hairs shiver on his forehead. Without a thought, she brushed her lips against his, pressed gently, closed her eyes and retreated to the door, opened it, walked through, closed it behind her and stood in the hallway where slow clouds of air chilled the sweat on her body.

She drove from the hospital with nerves of steel, knuckles white on the steering wheel, and ready for anything.

She saw him standing by the side of the road. He looked as though he were waiting for her car to pass and then he would continue on his way. On his head was a black floppy hat like Cliff's and its shadow hid most of his face. The shape of him seemed familiar. She braked slightly and tried to watch him without appearing to. She thought for a moment it *was* Cliff, but he was too small. Then she felt a surge of annoyance as she thought for a moment it was Daniel with Cliff's hat on, but as she passed him he whipped off the hat in one movement and held it out and waved it around. She saw his keen features behind a beard. Her foot skipped across the brake pedal and the car dipped and rocked and then she was past him and she looked in the mirror and saw him looking up the road after her, head tilted at a strange angle she knew, she knew, she knew. His name was dead and cold on the tip of her tongue.

Her foot found the accelerator and pressed it as far to the floor as it would go.

I remember a child walking through the garden, along pathways through flowerbeds, face upturned and squinting at the sun, running on sturdy legs across the grass, becoming giddy watching a dragonfly floating through the air. I called to her as dizziness tripped

*her feet and sent her tumbling, white arms still spinning, looking
at me for a moment in surprise before her eyes overflowed.*

*I can't for the life of me remember her name even though I know
it's as close to me as my own.*

Days or weeks or months later—he had no way of telling—
Cliff sat in the sun on a bench in the hospital garden. He
smoked and waved away flies with seamless patience. The
plaster on his arm had split and borne a pale arm. His fingers
were whiter than they had ever been; all the grime gone, all
the oil.

He sat and studied the horizon. The lighthouse could have
been the twinkling tip of something dreaming deep in the
cool earth. The sea was absolutely calm.

An old man set up an easel out on the hospital lawn and
started to paint. Cliff watched him and then, curious, wandered over to see what he was painting.

A silver river ran like vapour through a forest. It was filled
with trailing green reeds and silver-skinned fish were jumping
from the water. Cliff smiled and turned his head. He remembered fishing with his grandfather. The image was as clear as
the painting. Intent on the water as young children are.
Dangling their hands in it; leaning over the side and driving
their grandfather to distraction. He was old even then. Watching fish jump from the water and then the big pull of a fish
and his grandfather yanking on the rod and the fish dazzling
and flipping in the sun and his grandfather yelling, 'Get the
net! Get the net! The net boy!' and he had leant over and tried
to scoop the fish out of the river but then the rod had flicked
out straight and the flashing silver fish had gone and instead
there was a hook flying through the air and then a jab and a
pull and the hook sliding into the flesh between his thumb
and finger, the barbed point driving in and upwards and him

looking at it wide-eyed, the pain waiting for him to think it was over before it began. Red blood welling from his hand like juice and he had stared at the hook as his grandfather kept shouting. The hook's smooth steel shaft protruding from his skin like the tail of a gleaming insect. He remembered being pleased when Susan turned white and fainted.

A pavilion of cloth like silk had sprung up from the grass near the river and flags, pennants and streamers fluttered gently in the breeze.

'I don't see that,' Cliff said.

'I should hope not, sunshine. Here, have a go.'

Cliff sat down and picked up the brush. He felt a hand on his back. The hand stroked tense muscles.

He looked around at the owner of the hand. It was the man with baby pink skin on his nose.

'Not you again, you bastard.'

'You should give those up.' The old man pointed to the cigarette in Cliff's hand.

'Get stuffed.'

Cliff held the brush in his right hand and looked at the picture. There was nowhere to start. As he looked, a black speck the size of a pinhead appeared in the sky over the river. He peered at it and the closer he was to the canvas the bigger it seemed to grow. He squinted and then the speck in the sky became a man. The man squinted back at him.

Cliff jumped up off the stool.

'Shit!' he said.

'Look,' the old man said, 'keep looking, you've missed something else!' He waved his hand past the canvas and seemed to point down the valley to the sea.

'What? Where? I don't see anything.'

'Here,' he said, and took the glasses from Cliff's face and polished them on his sleeve.

'There, can you see now? Down at the gate there!'

'Oh, yeah, now I can. Who's that?'

'Someone you know, I think.'

A honey-coloured beam of light, as soft as anything, stretched across the sky like something he could walk on.

He knew who it was. He hesitated.

'Well, go on, do you want me to carry you or something?'

'No thanks, mate. I can walk.'

He walked across the broad sweep of green grass with his arms swinging at his sides. He walked until the gate stopped him and he reached through it and, with a shaking hand, touched the person standing there on the other side.

BRACELET HONEYMYRTLE
Judith Fox

Shortlisted in the *Australian*/Vogel Literary Award

'Wonderfully sustained . . . the sense of fulfilment achieved in simple reflection is marvellous.'

Jill Kitson

'A splendid, moving book.'

Andrew Riemer

Annie Grace is an old woman. She tends her garden, and cares for a baby, her great great-niece, Kimberley. It is a quiet life.

Born into a strict Christian family in Sydney at the start of the century, Annie contends with an overbearing mother and a harsh religion. Yet something stirs under the starch of faith. Annie finds a friend late in life and discovers a passion for living to equal her passion for gardening. In her sixties, Annie confronts her mother.

This is the story of one woman's struggle to lay claim to her own life. And within the seemingly narrow contours of family and church and garden, Annie discovers that it is, after all, a big life.

1 86373 850 9

CREW
Tony McGowan

Highly Commended in the *Australian*/Vogel
Literary Award

'Such an insight into sporting machismo that
it demands to be published.'

Jill Kitson

'A forceful, convincing articulation of blokes,
sport, mateship and the pleasures of pain.'

Marele Day

Set against a polluted summer on Sydney
beaches in the late 1980s, the gleaming
image of the bronzed Aussie lifesaver is
stripped away to reveal the melanoma scars,
sea ulcers and beer gut.

Through the eyes of gentle giant Derrick, we
join the crew of the Argo as they bump
through the rugged waters of surfboat
rowing, encountering wild boozers, yobbo
pranksters, shipwrecks, giant waves and sea
monsters—all in their quest for the fabled
gold medal.

1 86373 848 7

THE HAND THAT
SIGNED THE PAPER
Helen Demidenko

Winner of the *Australian*/Vogel Literary
Award

'A searingly truthful account of terrible
wartime deeds that is also an imaginative
work of extraordinary redemptive power.'
Jill Kitson

'Astonishingly talented . . . with the true
novelist's gift of entering into the
imagination of those she is writing about.'
David Marr

The Hand that Signed the Paper tells the
story of Vitaly, a Ukrainian peasant, who
endures the destruction of his village and
family by Stalin's communism. He welcomes
the Nazi invasion in 1941 and willingly
enlists in the SS Death Squads to take a
horrifying revenge against those he perceives
to be his persecutors.

This remarkable novel, a shocking story of
the hatred that gives evil life, is also an
eloquent plea for peace and justice.

1 86373 654 9

A MORTALITY TALE
Jay Verney

Shortlisted in the *Australian*/Vogel Literary Award

'Like flood, heat, age and guilt this book creeps up on you—forcing you to take notice.'

Jennifer Rowe

One rainy night Vincent Cusack appears, briefly, lit up for one final, fatal moment in the headlights of Carmen Molloy's car. Carmen is unquestionably an honourable woman, yet is able to drive on home and to be apparently shocked and saddened by news the next day of Vincent's untimely death.

In an exceptionally witty, perceptive and challenging literary debut, Jay Verney teases readers with fascinating 'What if?' questions as Carmen hosts Vincent's wake, avoids police questioning, battles a chorus of internal voices—and promises herself she can get away with the most disturbing of crimes.

1 86373 669 7

SOLSTICE
Matt Rubinstein

Shortlisted in the *Australian*/Vogel Literary Award

'An exuberant inside look at Australian youth culture . . . Amazingly, a first novel in Vikram Seth's demotic mode.'

Judith Rodriguez

'An Oz Midsummer Nights Dream, witty tender and erudite.'

Rhyll McMaster

Twenty-four hours in mid-summer Adelaide. A city seething with vitality at a microscopic level. A vibrant patchwork of individuals, colourful and unique. Twenty-four hours of love lost, and found in instant passion, or travel and adventure, captured and transformed in verse which leaps, and tricks to race and stop the clock.

The characters? In their talented and tormented twenties: their stories told in a beautiful and different way.

A brilliant literary debut that will inevitably be likened to Vikram Seth's *Golden Gate*—and is as vivid and refreshing.

1 86373 723 5

THE MULE'S FOAL
Fotini Epanomitis

Winner of the *Australian*/Vogel Literary
Award

In one despairing moment Theodosios
abandons his wife and gorilla child and then
spends a lifetime trying to get them back.
But what's a lifetime in a place like this?

Here nothing belongs to you—not even your
grief. People steal your letters and gossip
your thoughts before you've spoken them.
And when they're desperate—and at some
point everyone is desperate—they go to the
whorehouse . . .

From the centre of chaos, Mirella, the
ancient whore, finds a calm place to tell this
unforgettable, timeless tale.

1 86373 454 6